MW01170742

Manifesto Destination

"Alec Cizak finds the naked truth on the printed page. An artist with no fear and thankfully no moral center."

—David Cranmer,
editor of *Beat to a Pulp*

"The city of Indianapolis like you haven't seen it before (at least not yet), seasoned with a splash of noir, a dash of dystopia and almost but not quite hard-boiled. More like Eggs Benedict—though that breakfast was originally invented as a hangover cure, and this might cause one. Alec Cizak's heady mixture of sci-fi and PI, bad cops and Big Brothers, is a dark, funny read, full of twists and a barely controlled rage at the state of our corporate nation. And by nudging his detective story into a disturbing but recognizable future, the author paints this concoction with an extra layer of despair, as we realize his Phil Dickian satire of manipulation is not just familiar, but also inevitable. Best read with Charlie Parker in the background (the hero probably wore out his 'Charlie Parker With Strings' tape, but it weaves the perfect soundtrack). Jazzy and weird, the whole thing is probably a thinly-veiled threat, but I had too much fun to heed any warnings. See you at the Magic Carpet before they tear it down."

—David James Keaton,
author of *Fish Bites Cop*

MANIFESTO DESTINATION

Other Titles by Alec Cizak

Between Juarez and El Paso
Crooked Roads
Down on the Street

ALEC CIZAK

MANIFESTO DESTINATION

All Due Respect
An imprint of Down & Out Books
3959 Van Dyke Rd, Ste. 265
Lutz, FL 33558
www.DownAndOutBooks.com

Cover design by Eric Beetner

ISBN: 1-946502-96-0
ISBN-13: 978-1-946502-96-4

To Mrs. Walker, my fourth grade teacher.
She taught me many hard lessons about the
consequences of challenging authority.

INTRODUCTION

"Order up!"

In some literary circles, genre fiction commands the same kind of respect as American fast food, complete with the grease-stained wrapper. It's considered un-healthy. Unpalatable. But most of all, *cheap*, as in pro-duced for the masses like so many Quarter-Pounders (or Double-Doubles, if you live closer to the West Coast).

By contrast, "literary" fiction is considered genre*less*, and therefore superior. "Mainstream," they sometimes call it. Slice-of-Life. Mood-Pieces. Quaint little ditties appearing in *The New Yorker*, often politically charged, and flaunting their lack of functioning plot as a virtue.

"What?" they say. "You want a plot? How *crass*. How *formulaic*."

Of course, some blue-collar writing-stiff can point out just how much genre fiction sells in comparison to the other kind. Which brings up fiery debates about the reading public's taste, the encroachment of best-selling giants like *Twilight* and *The Hunger Games* into mass consciousness, Western Civilization's cultural decline, the evils of texting, etc., etc.

It gives academics something to do.

The PI genre, in particular, is often relegated to the

lowest of the low, that bottom-shelf of cliché-ridden hackwork they warn you about in books on proper fiction writing. It gets sneered at. English majors working as baristas will point out how private investigator stories, sometimes given the tag "hardboiled," are in reality poor cousins to the much more emotionally-encompassing "noir" works, which have a French word to describe how profound they are.

Whatever, buddy. Just leave me some room at the top for cream.

This is all to say that good writing is where you find it, and that can be damn near anywhere; genre, mainstream, on bathroom walls, page 23 of your daughter's *My Little Pony* fan-fic manuscript, what-have-you. If genre fiction is comfort food, then, well, that's because it's comfortable. The world needs Roger Corman as much as Truffaut.

Which brings me to Alec Cizak. If you've ever read his blog *No Moral Center* (and he likes to kid about how many people have), then you know he's made the elevation of genre fiction his tent-pole. He's done more than talk about it, in fact: in 2010 he began the online fiction magazine *All Due Respect* as an outlet for writers produc-ing quality crime fiction. He expanded to include several fiction genres in his next project, the print magazine *Pulp Modern*, which continues to this date with issue #5. And in 2012, he released the ambitious *Uncle B's Drive-In Fiction*, a whopping softcover with no less than six novel-las crammed inside, all extoling the Grade-B subject matter associated with that vanishing (vanished?) institu-tion of the title.

What you have in your hands now is *Manifesto Destination*, a solid example of the PI genre dusted with dystopian science-fiction elements, and set in the unlikely location of Indianapolis. Elmore Johnson is the novel's protagonist, a shutterbug with a penchant for Jim Bean and a .38 named after his homicidal first wife. Like all good PI stories, *Manifesto* follows a crooked path of betrayal and deception, though it does so against a larger backdrop, exploring themes of social class, ethnicity, nostalgia, addiction, and the all-encompassing tentacles of Big Pharmacy. Written in 2001, the novel has a subversive and eerily prescient feel. No spoilers, but you likely won't see the end coming.

Alec's talent embraces the literary side of fiction without being smug about it. His no-nonsense delivery can wax poetic, as when he describes a jazz tune playing on Elmore's outdated tape-deck: "Charlie Parker scattered notes like frantic bumble bees throughout my car." Or it can delve right to the heart of classic tough-guy narrative: "I removed my hand and let him know I'd punch him if he thought better of keeping his yapper at room temperature."

Beautiful stuff, no matter what side of the cultural aisle you're on.

So take the plunge, citizen. *Manifesto Destination* goes down easier than a men's magazine from the '60s or '70s—and it doesn't need a brown paper wrapper to hide behind.

Garnett Elliot,
2013

1

Her name was Felicia. We had a history, better days. Now she just used me to snap pictures of bad people doing bad things for her underground newspaper, *Little Brother*. I didn't think much of it when she called me and asked if I still had my camera.

"Sure, baby." The sweet talk annoyed her. Mostly because once upon a time it worked. "Come on over."

My office was on 38th and New Jersey, across from an apartment building filled with working folk caught in the routine. When I was bored, which tended to coincide with the lack of a bottle, I watched the dramas play out. Dad or Mom got home from work, bushed, agitated, the kids pushed that last button and the wailing started. Sometimes the cops joined in.

The window directly across from mine, however, had been empty for as long as I could remember. Maybe the room was haunted. Maybe it just smelled like bad memories. Whatever the reason, the slumlord handing out keys in that joint couldn't give one away.

I owned three tapes of music. *Charlie Parker With Strings* was in my car. The other two were John Coltrane albums, copied from long play vinyl records, complete with the comfortable pops of dust and scratches. I put the first one, *Sun Ship*, in my ancient radio and cassette combo. I shuffled through my desk. Maybe I was anxious to see Felicia.

Lorraine, my snub nosed .38, sat in the flat upper drawer. There were two filing drawers on the side, the top holding my camera, lens case, and rolls of film. The bottom contained my best friend, Jim Beam. I took the bottle out and snagged a swig just as Felicia knocked on the door.

"It's open!" I reached into my pocket and pulled out a case of Apache cigars. Four for a dollar. You couldn't beat it if you tried. As Felicia walked in, I lit one and put the booze away.

"How's things?" Felicia was packed tight in a mini-skirt and striped T-shirt to match. When she walked, she had to corkscrew on account of a pair of heels lifting her half a foot off the ground. She had shoulder-length hair, braided, and she smelled like caramel candy. In the ten years I had known her, she hadn't aged a day. She sat in the chair on the opposite side of my desk. It was the only other place to sit, besides maybe the desktop, or my worn-down bed, shoved to the side of the room.

"You got some work?" I leaned forward and exhaled away from her eyes. The sun beat in behind me, turning the smoke a rich blue that swirled around the room according to wind provided by a standing fan in the corner opposite my bed.

"I wouldn't be here for anything else."

"That hurts."

"Give me a break." She rummaged through a plastic handbag she probably called a purse. "What happened between us was an accident."

"So you're saying lightning doesn't strike twice?"

She found a picture in her bag and slid it across the desk. "Don't flatter yourself." She looked around, like someone wishing they were in a bigger room. "You got a beer?"

I nodded toward the rusted up fridge by the door. It came with the place, probably there when the building was built in 1922. Beer wasn't my preference, but I kept some around for the hell of it.

As Felicia helped herself to a can of Schlitz, I looked over the photo. It was a graduation shot of a cute blond-haired blue-eyed girl. Her smile suggested she had never starved a day in her life. "Who's the princess?"

Felicia sat back down, took a swig of beer and frowned. "You can't even figure out the difference between a healthy brew and piss." She paused and then took another sip. "The girl's name is Marsha Black, daughter of Leonard Black."

"Leonard Black? Doesn't he own…"

"Express Taxi. At least, that's what he doesn't mind the public knowing. He's also the CEO of Daisy Chemical. You have to dig to find that out. Any man hiding his credentials like that can only be one thing: corrupt."

"Now, now, let's not jump to any conclusions."

"Put a sock in it, Elmore Johnson. There's a reason you're the last resort for anyone looking for a snoop. Black is a gangster. He's also one of the most feared men in this city, politically. I want to know why. Lucky for us, his daughter is a typical white girl—wild as hell."

"There's nothing typical about that. You should see some of the white girls I dated in my time. I'd hold their hands to make sure they still had a pulse."

"Like Lorraine?" Felicia raised her left brow. "All she ever did was try to shoot you in bed."

3

"What'd you go and bring her up for?"

Felicia stood. "She's the reason I left you, Elmore. She's the reason you've lost every good woman you've ever had a chance with." She moved toward the door. "Pay is the usual. You can find Ms. Black at the Magic Carpet Lounge."

"What's she do there?"

Felicia opened the door. "What do you think, Einstein?"

I watched her leave. It wasn't the first time. Wouldn't be the last. Felicia Hill was the finest journalist in Indianapolis, a model troublemaker, and a hell of a woman. And I had had her, for good. I said "Lorraine" one time too many in my sleep, with Felicia next to me, and that was that.

I opened the flat drawer, took the pistol out, pointed it at my head and considered finishing the job. When the real Lorraine tried to snuff me, I wrestled the gun away from her. It went off and the bullet punctured her heart.

I walked into my bathroom, which was also my kitchen and my darkroom. In the corner underneath the sink, by the toilet, I kept my photography equipment—three bins for chemicals and a developing lamp. On the other side of the sink, by the tub, I stored dishes, pots, pans, a microwave, coffee machine and table-top burner. It was crowded, but I didn't make the kind of money in a year that allowed luxuries like space to breathe. I took some dirty plates out of the sink, turned the water on and splashed my face. Catching my reflection in the mirror, I made eye contact and then got the hell out of there as soon as possible.

2

Just south of Monument Circle, the center of Indianapolis, the Magic Carpet Lounge sat on a strip of land between Meridian and Illinois Street. The red-bricked building was bordered by neon outlines of naked women. Real classy. The only thing fancier than the outside was the inside.

The stage occupied the entire middle of the bar. On a good night, as many as five ladies at a time took their clothes off and acted happy for a buck or two. Well-mannered perverts from around the city parked their snouts along the perimeter and drooled.

The altar drinks were shoved across was at the front of the joint and just to the left of that was a row of couches. Any bozo with cash could lure a lady back there and sit still for the duration of a song while she worked up a sweat convincing the clown she liked him.

The Magic Carpet was the most famous strip club in the city. Broken girls from all over town strived to one day strut the blue catwalk and straddle one of three poles lining the center of the stage.

I showed up around midnight. That's when the dedicated perverts made their move for a permanent position gnawing on their favorite girls' ears until closing. Marsha

Black was dancing when I arrived. She jiggled in a pink nighty and a pair of sheer undies. I sat down at a table near the stage. A waitress asked me if I needed a drink.

"That's a dumb question." I cupped my hand near her ear to make sure she understood exactly what I needed. "Whiskey and water. Don't skimp on the juice. Tell the barkeep to use Jim Beam. Don't waste my time with that crap in the well."

The waitress looked confused.

I held up three fingers. "Whiskey," I said. Then, holding up one finger, I concluded: "Water."

She shuffled off to relay my order to the bartender.

Meanwhile, Ms. Black removed her nighty and nuzzled a businessman's nose between her artificially-sculpted breasts.

What was a rich, well-to-do girl like that doing in a place like the Magic Carpet? I scooted closer. Marsha had dirty brown and yellow scars on her arms. Daddy's little princess was doing drugs. Heroin, I guessed.

The lucky gal who didn't have to take her clothes off that night brought me my drink. I held her at my table while I tried it. The bartender had gotten it right. I smiled, handed her a ten and told her to keep the change.

Two heavy metal songs came and went and Marsha Black was relieved of dancing on the stage. She wound her way through the crowd of gawkers. She got to me before anyone had the courage to ask her for a romp on the couches.

"How are you tonight?" She plopped her perfect tush on my lap.

I looked into her eyes. They were ocean blue, the kind that made you think of exotic islands you'd never

6

get a chance to visit. For all her posturing and putting on that she was a grown woman, deep in the back of her pupils I detected the reflection of innocence, like an inhabiting spirit, drifting toward oblivion. Somebody broke her heart, in the worst way, and she was dead set on getting revenge. Trouble was, the only person she was hurting was herself. I could have told her all that, sure, but what if the dummy listened? Then I'd be out five grand.

"Doing great," I said. I tipped my drink to show her my only true love.

She was determined to get something out of me so I pulled some cash from of my pocket and stuffed a dollar in her panties. That made her happy enough. She kissed me on the cheek, jumped off my lap and moved on.

I spent the next three hours watching Marsha Black and a dozen other girls just like her illustrate how meaningful their lives had become, over and over again.

The bar shut down at three o'clock in the morning. That was when the bouncers escorted the girls to their cars. A few of the ladies decided to take clients home and continue moving money in exchange for moving their bodies.

Little Marsha Black, dressed in a halter top and skin-tight jeans, strutted out. She was accompanied by two other girls. They looked as though they were a few years older, maybe working the Magic Carpet to get through college. All of them piled into a silver Caddie driven by a man my age. He was built like a football player and dressed in fancy night club gear, suggesting he was super important in the world of beer, breasts and loud rock and roll songs that all sounded the same.

I watched this from the comfort of my blue Town

Car, a dinosaur, like me, made in 1975 and passed from my father's hands to mine. It got me around the city without being noticed. The only fault in the frame was a cavity on the driver's side, by the headlights. Many years before—1993, to be exact—Lorraine spun off on one of her crazy binges and slammed the Lincoln into a fire hydrant.

I was parked in an alley between the post office and the Vonnegut Lofts, a renovated factory housing artists and other dreamers. South of all that was a satellite office of Daisy Chemical. Since the invention of Seraphim, a magic pill that made rain look like sunshine, Daisy had been expanding. They purchased the White Castle next to the Vonnegut Lofts. Rumors spread that the artists' haven was next to go. It was only a matter of time before Daisy gobbled up the Magic Carpet.

Once the Caddie was half a block away, I cranked the engine on the Towne Car and followed.

The driver took them up Illinois to the roundabout at Monument Circle. He veered right at Market and drove to Delaware. There, he turned the only way he could, left. Native residents of Indy used Delaware to go north when they weren't in the mood to sit in traffic. It was one way clear up to Fall Creek, five lanes, always moving, even during rush hour.

Delaware gradually illustrated how money had drifted north. After leaving the business district, the houses were one- or two-story numbers. Students or welfare cases lived on either side of the street. Once you got beyond 38th Street, it was mansion city.

At Fall Creek, the Caddie veered left onto Washington Boulevard. The driver was possibly headed to the Broad Ripple area. Anyone going further north would have turned right and cruised up to College, or maybe even Keystone.

The Caddie stopped at 42nd and Washington, directly across from a Greek church. I turned left and drove as though I were going to Pennsylvania Street. I made a right on Penn and pulled to the curb, turned my car off and got out.

Creeping around the corner, I watched the bouncing girls and driver enter a large three-story house on Washington. I ran back to my car, opened the trunk and retrieved my camera. After putting the longest lens on, a two-fifty, and loading film, I rushed to the mini-mansion.

Tall rose-bushes surrounded the outside. I saw no signs of dogs or other foul beasts watching over the joint. I crept up to a window with light coming through it. Peering inside, I saw that a large area, perhaps intended by the architect to be the living room, had been cleared for movie lights and a pair of small digital video cameras. The center of all this attention was a queen-sized bed. Free standing frames with curtain rods made up the backdrop, flowing with the help of two electric fans.

As the ladies and their giant escort walked into the room, five more men greeted them. Within no time, the order of tasks was revealed. Two of the new men went to work lighting the romantic set up by clipping red gels to the barn doors on the movie lamps. One of the fresh faces got cozy with the girls, taking them in his arms, talking them up, eventually convincing them to sit down on the bed and take their clothes off. How he managed this was beyond me. He was tall, lanky, and looked like the last time he had his hands on a woman was never.

The other two men got behind the cameras and put

the entire sequence on tape. The whole thing brought me back to my youth, a century ago, when movies like that were made with real cameras and compelling story lines. The good old days, as fossils sometimes expressed it.

Daddy's little girl appeared to have a problem. The two friends of hers from the Magic Carpet worked her body from every angle, but that didn't soften her up to the camera. The director called on the big guy who drove them there. He picked up a pouch resting on the floor by the entrance to the room and walked over to the festival of love on the bed.

The driver knelt, opened the works, and proceeded to fix up a needle of a yellow substance I had never seen. I snapped a few shots of the syringe getting stuck into Marsha's arm, her blood being drawn, mixed with the dope, and then plunged back into her vein.

Whatever it was, it worked wonders on the little princess because she lay back with a smile from ear to ear. I shot out the rest of the roll as the other two women worked Ms. Black into a frenzy that made the director applaud like a child at the circus.

By the time the auteurs were finished, the sun bled over the horizon. I decided I needed another drink.

I headed back to my car and drove to the Standard Foods on 38th Street, a twenty-four hour convenience store that had the decency to sell booze at five in the morning. My nostalgia for old fashioned pornography vanished as I downed a pint of Jim Beam on the drive back to my office.

3

Felicia showed up the next day at noon. She pounded on the door. The only reason I opened my eyes was because I knew she'd have a check for me. I sat up. I had fallen asleep in my pants. I put on a shirt and let her in.

She was dressed in a black skirt hugging her hips tight enough to reveal she wasn't wearing anything underneath. Her upper torso was barely covered by a flowery number showing off her belly button and the small of her back. I could see the border of a burgundy bra maintaining order. My bet was that she knew I would be hung over and she understood how to make that irrelevant.

"You look horrible," she said. She rushed past me and searched my desk for her pictures. "What the hell?"

"I didn't get home until six in the morning." I took her by the hand and led her to my bathroom.

The negatives from the previous night's work hung with clothes pins from a line drawn parallel with the curtain rod in the shower. Felicia stepped inside. I shut the door and turned on a red light.

"Don't get any ideas," she said.

"There ain't enough room to get much of anything in here." I smiled and winked, though I couldn't be sure she saw all that in the dim light.

I took down a strip of negatives illustrating Marsha Black's thespian activities from the house on Washington Boulevard. Felicia studied them and grinned.

"Nice," she said. She inched closer to me.

I let her have a gander at another strip, this one showing the little angel putting dope in her veins.

"Did you get any shots of her dancing?"

"You don't bring a camera into a strip joint. Not if you like using your legs to get around."

"Crap."

I worried she might skimp my take. "No fears." I put my arm around her, squeezed her shoulder to comfort her. "You got enough material here to cause a little ruckus."

She shrugged. "I suppose." Reaching into her bra, she pulled out a check.

"Thank you."

"I want the best pictures of her shooting up." Felicia rubbed her chin, as though she had a better choice. "A few more of the party on the bed. I'll be back by six this evening. I only have to hustle the lunch shift today, which is good because I have a deadline tomorrow night."

"You working the Rise and Shine Cafe?"

"I quit that gig," she said. "I'm over at Denny's now."

"Really?" I was a Grand Slam junky. "The one on Michigan Avenue?"

"No." She fumbled for the door.

I turned the red light off and we moved back into my office. Felicia headed for the door, shot through without even saying good-bye.

I sat at my desk, opened the bottom drawer, pulled

out the whiskey and took a swig. A half-burnt Apache cigar was propped over the side. I picked it up, lit it and considered what I might have had for breakfast if that sort of thing fit into my routine. Then I tilted my head back and passed out once more.

4

Around two in the afternoon, I was brought back to the conscious world by a bastard named Jerome McElroy. He was a cop. Vice and, whenever the money was good, narcotics. He woke me up by dumping the rest of the whiskey in my bottle over my head.

I rubbed booze out of my eyes. "What's up, buddy?"

We were old friends. Jerome was the reason I lost my job with the Indianapolis Police Department. He set up an operation where he and his boys in vice controlled the exchange of money for sex along Washington Street. By the time I stumbled onto their network, they were in charge of the entire east side. An amazing accomplishment. When the issue of *Little Brother* came out with my pictures of IPD officers taking money from hookers, the brass at City-County decided I was the bad guy and found a no-talent hack to replace me and take crime photos for them.

Jerome shoved a picture under my nose. It was Marsha Black, same studio shoot, apparently, that provided the snapshot Felicia had shown me the day before. "You seen this little chunk of ass?"

I shook my head.

Jerome nodded to a young cop he brought with him.

I had never met him before so I assumed he was working his way up the ladder of corruption. He couldn't have asked for a better mentor. The kid traipsed over and cracked me in the face with the back of his hand.

Leaning closer, Jerome smiled and asked, in a nicer voice, "You seen her, Elmore?"

My bathroom door was closed. I couldn't remember if I had shut it after showing my work to Felicia. Regardless, the cop knew better. I shrugged. "Maybe I run into her once or twice, or just once, sure."

"You want to work with us, Elmore." Jerome walked around my desk, reached down and pulled out the flat drawer. He took Lorraine in his hand. "I'll hold onto this while we talk, if you don't mind."

"Relax."

He placed the gun on the desk, slowly, just far enough away from me that it wouldn't be an issue. "The whore's name is Marsha Black," he said. "Her dad owns Express Taxi, among other things. Says his little darling didn't show up for breakfast."

"You can look around if you like," I said. "If she was ever here, she's gone now."

The rookie stomped over and introduced his knuckles to my face one more time. I felt blood trickle from my nose. It wouldn't have bothered me, but I only had one towel and didn't much care to filthy it up with more blood than usual.

"Bouncer at the Magic Carpet Lounge puts you there last night. Daddy's little girl just happened to be there as well. Bouncer says she sat on your lap for a buck."

"That's a pretty good eye," I said. I realized they hadn't seen the negatives in the bathroom.

"So you going to talk?"

"She put it in my face for a second. I gave her a cookie and she went to work on someone else."

Jerome stuffed his free hand in his pocket and leaned forward, raising his voice in the process. "This girl's dad can have you buried in a cornfield with a phone call." He shook a finger at me. "Don't be stupid."

McElroy and his shadow backed out of my office.

As soon as they were gone I stood, wiped my blood off on my undershirt, and got dressed.

I decided to finish Felicia's job early. I developed the pictures she asked for, put them in a folder and headed out the door.

5

Felicia lived in an apartment in the Sanders Housing Projects just off 25th Street and College Avenue. Her building was right on the parameter, meaning I didn't have to drive into the housing development to see her. I parked at the curb of 25th and Ralston, got out and stumbled toward her door. Along the way, several of Felicia's neighbors gave me dirty looks. I understood, believe me; I hadn't showered in at least a week.

She lived in Apartment C3. I rang her buzzer. It took her a second.

"Yes?"

"Let me in."

"Elmore?"

"That's right."

I walked up the stairs and knocked on her door. When she opened it I heard the shrieking of her five-year-old son, Tony. Tony was autistic. Rather than having him doped up in a home or hospital, Felicia had taken on the task of raising him all by herself.

"What's up?" she asked.

I handed her the folder with the pictures. "There you

go."

Felicia took the photos out, looked at them and smiled. "You're a saint."

"Yesterday I was a scumbag. Make up your mind."

She floated to her kitchen, reached into her fridge, a great deal nicer than mine, and pulled out a bottle of Guinness. "Need anything to drink?"

"Whiskey and water," I said. I had to raise my voice above the screams of Tony, seated on the floor smashing toy trucks into each other. "Don't skimp on the juice. Give me three fingers."

"All I have is water." She brought me a glass that might as well have been empty. "There you go." She spoke in a tone she probably used on her little boy whenever it was time for mommy to do some thinking.

"I'm curious about one thing," I said. "How goddamn dumb do you think I am?" I knew she hadn't kidnapped the princess, but I figured making my opinion more drastic than it was might shake the truth from her a bit easier.

"What are you talking about?"

I grabbed her by her shoulders, just rough enough to let her know I wasn't in the mood to slosh through manure. "The cops came by today. It seems daddy's little girl is missing."

Felicia cupped her hand over mouth.

I nodded. "Why don't you do me the kind favor of telling me exactly what your angle on this is. You're not straight with me, the boys from IPD will no doubt show up the instant you publish those photos."

She thought about it, sizing up the story so far, then moved to her only window. Orange and yellow curtains kept the sunshine to a minimum. She peered through them. "Come here."

I joined her at the window. Below, a group of teen-agers was seated on the hood of one of those oversized station wagons folks with tiny wee-wee's drove to make themselves feel better. We stood there and watched them for some time. "What's the point?"

"Just chill."

Within five minutes, two cars rolled up. One fancy, filled with yuppies, the other a flatbed pickup driven by white folks who appeared to be on the brutal side of poverty. Both stopped at the SUV, had an exchange with the thuglets calling themselves "gangstas." Money was passed from one hand to another and vials of dust were doled out to the visitors, who then stepped on the gas and fled the projects.

"I know this routine, baby," I said. "It's a sad state of affairs and we're powerless to stop it. What the hell does it have to do with Marsha Black?"

"Be here tomorrow morning at five. Park somewhere you can't be seen. Wait for an Express Taxi to show up. That's what I'm trying to expose."

I walked away from the window. I couldn't make up my mind as to whether or not I trusted her.

"I'll pay you to tail that cab, all day tomorrow. What do you say?" She tried an innocent look on me. The only thing more pathetic than her attempt to use her big brown eyes to make me do what she wanted was the fact that I, a thirty-five-year-old man, still hadn't figured out a way to resist.

"Five grand," I said, harboring the belief that I had any power in the relationship.

"Of course."

Tony grew tired of smashing his trucks into each

other. He cried for his mother. Felicia picked him up.

"I have to work on the newspaper," she said, nodding toward her second bedroom which served as her office. Computers and printers and stacks of paper were crammed in with a desk she used to lay out *Little Brother*.

I realized for the first time that one of us was getting ripped off. I paid twice as much as she did for my bachelor's apartment. She had two bedrooms, a kitchen and a living room. Then I remembered what I had just witnessed through her window. You see, as shitty as my neighborhood seemed, people weren't allowed to deal dope in their front yards.

6

When I got back to my place I took my shirt off, plopped down on my bed with half a bottle of Jim Beam and listened to the radio. No word of Leonard Black's daughter missing. The only news worth remembering was a bit about a drug that was taking over the city. Nobody knew what it was, but the kiddies called it Stardust, and according to the drone reading the report over the air, it was giving them one hell of a trip.

Must be nice, I thought, taking a swig of whiskey. The entire newscast was sponsored, like everything else in Indianapolis, by Daisy Chemical. They constantly interrupted the jazz music my station played to remind me that Seraphim was the number one anti-depressant in the world.

I was snoring before the sun set.

7

I woke up at two. My mind was static. I needed food, a cigar, and more whiskey. I went into the bathroom, moved the trays with developing chemicals away from the toilet and threw up whatever scraps I put in my belly the day before. I stepped into the shower, turned it on, dunked my head and got back out.

Next to my refrigerator was a pile of clothes. Sifting through four different button-down shirts, I found one that smelled the least offensive and put it on. I decided to wear my black suit, complete with black tie.

Gathering up my camera and lenses, I stuffed two rolls of film in my pocket and hit the road.

Indy was a fickle town with little action that early or late, depending on what side of the day you closed your eyes. The only restaurants open were diners like Denny's or Perkins. The closest joint to my side of town was a Steak 'n Shake on 52nd and College. When I arrived, six cops were stuffed into the booth closest to the door. I parked myself at a table behind them.

After ordering a bowl of baked beans and a plate of fries, I leaned back to listen to the boys in blue. I caught the beginning of a conversation about this garbage they were calling Stardust.

"I pulled them over," said the man telling the story. He looked about thirty, probably on the force just long enough to realize he was a pawn in a game they'd never let him win. He saw me listening, figured I was nobody worth a worry and continued. "It's a girl driving and she's got her boyfriend in the passenger seat, who appears to be at least five years younger than she is. I shine the light on them, right, and neither one wants to look at me, so I ask them to step out." He took a sip of his coffee, made sure he still had his colleagues' attention. "Their pupils are huge, I mean, they looked like they might black out their eyeballs completely, so I put them up against their car. The girl, she's dressed in a high, high mini-skirt, so that when she's propped on the trunk, I can see her panties."

This elicited an enthusiastic response from the lot of them.

"I search the boy, then the girl, several times." He raised his eyebrows, demonstrating what Groucho Marx might have looked like if he had been a no good, corrupt douchebag. "When I go through her purse, I find two bottles of the stuff."

"Stardust?" The youngest in the group, wide-eyed from the presence of the veteran pork sitting around him, double-checked to make sure he was following the story properly.

"Right, right. Now, we all know that the boy probably bought the dope, gave it to her to hold on to, but he sees the vials and pretends he's some holy Roman Catholic who's just seen a grown woman naked for the first time. I ask, 'who does this belong to?' The girl, of course, looks to her little comrade to bail her out, and he just shrugs."

"What a pig," one of the other cops said.

My food arrived. I ate quietly, so as not to miss Officer Friendly's tale of drugs and panties.

"She starts balling, I mean crying like her best friend just bought the frigging farm. I let both of them know that, as of that point, *she's* under arrest. The spineless male twat raises his hands and tells her, get this, he tells her, 'I didn't think you were like that,' so she just looks him dead in the eye and says..."

The waitress stood over their table with a fresh pot of coffee. Had she a tray of donuts in her other hand, no doubt, one of them would have asked her to marry him.

"Anyway," the storyteller continued, "when we get this stuff back to the lab, they say it's brand new. No other city has it, yet."

They all nodded on the word "yet," as though it were inevitable that a fad in Indianapolis would eventually infect the rest of the country.

I finished up my fries and beans, drank my water and headed for the cashier. Before I could make it out the door, one of the older cops recognized me.

"Elmore Johnson?" He had a grin on his face like a schoolyard bully looking for someone to donate lunch money.

"What's it matter?" It was past four in the morning, I was running late and the last thing I needed was a confrontation with the police.

"How's the picture business?" The whole lot of them busted up laughing. You'd of thought they just heard the funniest joke in the world.

As I exited the joint, I caught site of my reflection in

the glass on the door. Maybe I was something to laugh at. I jumped in my Towne Car and sped to the nearest Village Pantry.

8

The so-called convenience store was out of Jim Beam. I settled for Mad Dog, only because I knew it would remind me how much better real whiskey is than anything else on the planet. They did have Apaches, though they only sold them one at a time. I bought two at a buck a piece.

I parked by a trash bin down the street from Felicia's building. Not too many people were awake. I figured my presence wouldn't be detected. I put the Charlie Parker tape in the twenty-five-year-old factory-provided deck which, thank you very much, still worked. I lit a cigar and worked on the bottle of Mad Dog.

Just after five o'clock, Express Taxi number 525 pulled up to the spot the kids selling dope had been the previous day. A tall, razor thin character, dressed in cut off sweats and a T-shirt, ran out of Felicia's building to greet the cab.

I picked up my camera and snapped a few shots of the exchange.

The cabbie, a white man in his forties, handed the younger man a black duffle bag. Junior then slid a wad of money into the cabbie's hand. They tossed some words back and forth and the taxi took off. The youngster toted the bag of goodies back inside.

OK, I thought, so Felicia was right about the cab bringing dope into the neighborhood. That still didn't reveal what the hell she expected to do with pictures of Leo's daughter. I was beginning to suspect Felicia's intentions were less journalistic and leaned more toward blackmail. Most of the work I did was used for that reason, though rich folks often went to court to play out a drama that conveniently avoided that dirty little word.

I threw the Lincoln into drive and followed the cab out of the projects. The taxi drove to college and turned left, toward downtown. As Charlie Parker scattered notes like frantic bumble bees throughout my car, I maintained a steady distance between me and the yellow chariot.

At Eastern Avenue the driver turned right. He turned left at Penn and continued south. Pennsylvania became Madison Avenue and, at an underpass leading to the corporate headquarters of Daisy Chemical, the cabbie turned left again and parked in a circular drive in front of the building.

I pulled to the curb underneath the bridge leading to the high rise. Stepping out, I dropped some coins in the meter and sat down on a concrete wall lining the side of the road.

The cabbie hustled into the building. I snapped a few pictures of him disappearing inside the revolving door. He was in the joint for no more than ten minutes before shuffling back out with a brand new duffle bag, just like the one he handed off to the kid at Felicia's place.

The cabbie drove from Daisy to a poor white neighborhood on the south side of town. He passed Fountain Square, on Virginia Avenue, and turned left on Naomi.

The taxi stopped in front of a dry-cleaners on the corner. A large man with stringy hair, wearing a leather jacket with a skull and the words "God Hates You" hand-drawn on the back, stepped out to greet the cabbie. They traded words and money for the duffle bag.

I photographed the whole thing. It dawned on me that I was sticking my feet in something I could very well drown in.

The cabbie repeated the routine several more times. I'd follow him to Daisy, then to a poor neighborhood. By noon he must have had enough money to quit the hack racket. I wondered how much of the bread was actually his to keep.

That question was answered around two in the afternoon. The cabbie dropped off a bag near Massachusetts Avenue, turned around and drove down Alabama to Market Street. He parked his car in a space that was clearly identified as a tow away zone for anyone other than law enforcement. Then he strolled into the twenty-story structure known as the City-County Building.

The City-County Building housed courts and cops and everything in between. There was even a morgue in the basement. One of the chief coroners was an old girlfriend of mine, Margaret Crumb. Basically, the building centralized the entire police operation. Before you went to lock-up in Indy, you paid a visit to the friendly clerks on Alabama and Market.

I parked my car and fed another meter and then sat on a bench outside the City Market, which was directly across the street from the door the cabbie had walked through. He spent about twenty minutes inside, then returned, got in his cab and took off once more.

I followed him from there to I-70 East. He got off at

Holt Road and pulled into the Express Taxi lot. Hundreds of cabs were parked on the west side of the building. The dispatch house and garage were just to the right of that. A set of gas pumps sat in between them. There was a line of parking spaces outside the dispatch building where, I assumed, cabbies paying their rent parked.

Except our friend in 525 pulled around to the front of the building, where picture windows suggested clerical and management types spent their days earning a much easier dollar. 525 was, in fact, the only cab parked on that side.

The driver got out and marched through the front door.

I stopped in at a McDonald's across the street. I was almost out of film. When the cabbie emerged once more, I shot out the roll and considered calling it a day.

Then I noticed the cabbie flipping through a stack of money in his chubby paws. The smile on his face told me that was his take. I glanced over to the side of the building taking care of the drivers who had to earn their money the hard way. It didn't seem fair to me. I decided to have a chat with the golden hack.

Calling from a pay phone inside the McDonald's, I ordered a taxi. "I'd like a particular cab," I told the dispatch lady. "Number 525, if that's possible." She put me on hold.

When the operator came back, she asked me, "Sir, where are you located?"

I hung up, but it was too late. Two cop cars passing the McDonald's on Holt stopped, their sirens flashed and they roared into the parking lot. I raced out the opposite door and ran to my Town Car.

As I cranked the engine, I turned around to look

inside the restaurant. The cops were conversing with a teenager behind the counter. I put the car in reverse and, as casually as possible, pulled into traffic. In my rear-view mirror I saw the officers walk out and glance around for, presumably, the drunk in the blue Lincoln. There were enough cars between me and the range of their naked eyes, however, to prevent them from catching sight of me.

I made my way back to my place on 38th Street. As far as I was concerned, Felicia was either going to have to ante up every reason she had for getting me involved in this situation, or she was going to have to give me a whole lot more money.

9

When I got back to my cage, I headed straight for my darkroom. I didn't even bother to lock the front door when I closed it. It was only after I had put my camera down on the toilet seat that I noticed something different about my apartment.

I peered around the bathroom door. There were two young gorillas in suits standing over an old monster seated in the chair on the business side of my desk.

"Mr. Johnson, I presume?" He spoke with a country accent, and not the kind that suggested saintly folks who plowed fields for a living.

I already knew who it was, but in my office, I was the only celebrity worth recognizing without any formal introduction. "Yes?" I feigned as much disinterest as possible.

"My name is Leonard Black. My friends call me Leo." He took a cigar case out of the breast pocket of his white suit, opened it, and produced a Cuban that probably cost more than my rent. He lit it, then completed his thought—"You can call me Mr. Black."

"What can I do for you?" I looked in my bathroom, noting whether or not Leo and his boys had removed the negatives of his little princess. They were still hanging from the clothespins over the tub. Idiots, I thought.

31

"You may or may not know, I have a daughter. Marsha. Rebellious. She was just graduated from high school this spring and damned if she's not sowing enough oats to populate a small country, if you catch my drift."

"She likes to smile, sure, I get the picture." I stopped myself from saying anything else.

"Marsha failed to come home this morning. I've been getting a lot of flack from a hundred different organizations lately. I don't know if she's been kidnapped, run away, or what."

"They got drones in uniforms for that sort of thing."

"No good, no good. The police can't help me unless I fill out an official report. Then the press would get wind and, well, I don't like publicity that doesn't paint a favorable portrait of me and my family."

I wondered if he ever ventured into the Magic Carpet while his daughter inspired naughty portraits in the minds of drunks and businessmen alike. "I usually don't work missing person cases, Mr. Black."

"I'm prepared to make an offer you'll find difficult to resist."

I raised an eyebrow, pretended to be interested.

"How does one million dollars sound to you?"

"She's worth that much to you? Noble."

"This is no joke, son." He clenched his fist, then took a drag off his cigar to calm down. "I don't want anyone to know about this."

"I got no friends." I told him. "In that respect, I guess I am the perfect man for the job. When do I get the money?"

Leo reached into the coat pocket opposite the one with the Cubans and produced a check. He placed it on the desk. It was for half a million.

"The rest," he said, "will be delivered upon your revealing her whereabouts."

"What if she's nowhere to be found? What if she's dead? What if she doesn't want to be found?"

He put his free paw over the check. "Do your best to make sure it's none of the above." He took his hand away and eased back into the chair.

"All right, Mr. Black. I'll sniff around."

"Very good." For the first time, the old man smiled. He stood and directed his goons to follow him out the door. Before shutting it, he turned around and added, "Part of that fee goes toward your word that you won't moonlight while working this case."

I realized I had taken jobs on both sides of a conflict I had yet to figure out. "Sure," I said.

He waited until he was certain he had my full attention. "You work for me, son, no one else."

Before I could respond, he shut the door. I wondered if he had seen the photos, if all he really wanted was insurance that I'd never show them around town.

Sitting down at my desk, I opened my favorite drawer. The bottle was empty. I had one cigar left. I lit it, leaned back and looked at the vacant apartment across the street. I tried thinking. It was a tough task without my buddy Jim Beam.

I had enough money to flee the country, but decided instead to stick around. My curiosity, always an enemy, took over. It had been my experience to accept everything that happened to me as intended. Call it fate, call it God, call it Vishnu, call it Betsy for all I cared…The universe was a giant equation that could be narrowed down to one number, and damned if I would work against it.

10

I had to sew the pieces together and it seemed to me that the house of dirty movies on Washington Boulevard was the best place to start.

I parked by the Greek church, along 42nd Street. The first thing I noticed as I crossed Washington was a red Chevy Astro in the driveway. Absent two nights previous, it completely changed my impression of who actually lived in the fancy house.

The sun was slipping off toward the west. I snuck up to the same windows I peeked through two nights before. The movie set was no longer there. The room was filled with a couch, several lamps and tables and a television. A man and woman in their late fifties sat like zombies in front of the propaganda machine.

I crept around the house. It was the product of two well-fed yuppies who had no doubt punched a clock for thirty years. A light glowed from a window leading to the cellar.

In the basement, the auteur who directed the dirty movie sat at a computer. He was dressed in a button-down shirt, slacks, and thick glasses over his nose. Across from the desk was a bed. Magazines with half-naked girls on the covers littered the floor.

I moved to the next window, which led to what appeared to be the only other room in the basement. Glare from Junior's computer spilled in, barely illuminating it. What I could make out was a table with a row of barrels on top of it. Fumbling around the frame of the window, I slid a finger over the top of the inside, unhitched the latch and cracked it. Quiet as possible, I opened it and climbed through. There was about a nine-foot drop to the floor.

When I landed, I twisted my foot and let out a growl. The sounds of typing coming from the next room ceased. I braced myself against the wall by the door and waited for him to charge through.

The door opened and the auteur stepped in. He turned his head, saw the impression of me in the dark and started to say something. I grabbed him, put my hand over his mouth and gave him the score:

"I got pictures of you and your buddies playing doctor with teenage girls on dope. If you don't want mom and dad to know what you do when they go away, keep quiet and answer my questions as best you can."

He nodded. I removed my hand and let him know I'd punch him if he thought better of keeping his yapper at room temperature.

"Who are you?" he asked.

"Somebody who, at this point, holds the key as to whether or not you get to continue living with the folks or have to go out and find a real job."

"What do you want to know?"

The kid was too easy. "Turn on the light," I said, nodding toward the table with the barrels.

He found a bulb hanging from the ceiling and pulled the chain. Twenty watts revealed Junior's other hobby.

The barrels on the table were various stages of some drug or another's construction.

"What's for dinner?"

"Well…" He stared at his feet, thinking maybe they'd answer for him.

I stepped closer, clenched my fist and raised it.

"It's called Stardust."

"What's in it?"

"Methamphetamine and MDMA."

"Ecstasy?"

"Right. Also, just for good measure, we add a dash of pure cocaine to every batch."

Jesus, I thought. "That's three jolts in one."

"So?"

I grabbed him by his shirt collar. "You better explain what the hell is going on. Ma and Pa are just a shout away."

He shrugged. "What do you want to know?"

"Start by telling me about your movie studio. How do you manage to produce your fine films without the folks finding out?"

"After eight o'clock, they're dead for twelve hours. Mom swallows enough Valium to knock out an army and Dad has been shooting prescription morphine since he took three bullets in his right leg in Vietnam."

"How often do you make these movies?"

"Once a week," he said. "I kind of have to. I'm under contract."

"With who?"

"Internet site, called Indy Friends. All amateur, all locals."

"Who runs it?"

"Not sure. I had to cut a deal with the cops. They

busted me selling Stardust to an undercover at the Magic Carpet."

Inside, I smiled. Sometimes the wounds stitch themselves on their own. "How long ago was this?"

"About a month. We only just came up with Stardust. It's the most addictive composition I've ever seen. When we explained to the cops that we could get women to do anything for it, they forced us in to a deal with them."

"Who's us?"

"Me and a co-worker. Tom Burden. He's as old as my parents. I'm doing an internship at his office."

"Daisy Chemical?"

"How'd you know?"

"Wild guess," I said. "How about the girl, Marsha Black?"

"Who's that?"

I smacked him one time with the back of my hand. He jumped to the side.

"I film new girls every week, Mr., ah, what was your name?"

"Two nights ago you filmed three girls. One of them wasn't playing ball, so you put some of this crap in her arm and she cozy'd up real nice to your cameras."

"The blonde," he remembered. "She left with Abe Miller, one of the owners of the Magic Carpet. I don't ever keep track of the girls after they do a picture for me."

"Abe, eh?"

He nodded.

"What's your name?" I asked, inching toward the window.

"Why?"

I turned around and made like I'd walk back and slap

him around a few times.

"Aaron, Aaron Milton. Most people know me by my handle on the Internet, SpaceDog2112."

"One last thing, SpaceDog." I shoved an empty bucket toward the window and turned it upside down. "What's the name of the cop you made the deal with?"

"Jerome McElroy."

I climbed onto the bucket, hoisted myself up by a plumbing pipe bolted to the ceiling and swung my legs through the window. When I was outside, I leaned back in. "By the way, SpaceDog, this conversation never happened. I hear about it from anyone else, it'll be the last bad decision you make in this life."

"Yes sir."

It was time to visit the Magic Carpet again.

11

Downtown I found a nice spot under a streetlamp a half block south of the strip joint. I was parked next to the Vonnegut Lofts. A construction company had wrapped a fence around it. Signs were posted: *No Trespassing*.

While I staked out the Magic Carpet, three different artists showed up, dressed in black. They scaled the fence, broke into the five-story number and walked out with canvasses, paints, and other supplies. I guess the good folks at Daisy didn't even give the residents time to retrieve their belongings before evicting them.

At a quarter until four, I moseyed on down to the parking lot next to the club. Most of the ladies were filing out, getting in cars, fending off customers who wanted more than the menu had to offer. I worked on an Apache underneath a high-hat lamp hanging off the side of the building. Some of the girls took note, smiled, mostly because they didn't recognize me as one of the pigs at the trough throwing dollars at them.

Two dancers strolled out with Abe at ten past four. They walked toward his Caddie. I looked around, made sure nobody else was in sight. He opened the back door for the ladies. I made my move.

"Excuse me." I pulled Lorraine out of my jacket and

aimed her at his belly.

Abe raised his arms halfway. "You're making a mistake, whoever you are."

"Won't be the first time." I directed him to walk with me behind the car, away from the light on the street. "How'd you get involved with the dork shooting pornos over on Washington?"

"How do you think?" His attitude told me he wasn't too nervous about standing there with a gun on him.

"If I had a better clue I wouldn't be chatting with you. I'd be at home with a bottle of whiskey and my thoughts." I slapped him with my knuckles. Without Lorraine at my side, I would have been a bit more diplomatic, considering the man was twice my size. "I know you and McElroy are in on it."

"Cops don't make a whole lot of money. I used to work on the force, so believe me, I know."

"You're breaking my heart. Get to the point."

"Simple. McElroy needed to make some bread on the outside. I told him we could probably convince the girls to get nasty on film for some extra money. Internet made distribution a whole lot easier."

"That mean McElroy's not running girls off Washington Street anymore?"

"How do you know about that?" He angled his head to change the way light hit my face. "Holy mother of Jesus. You're the snoop."

"Good for you." I raised the gun, reminding him who would decide when class was dismissed. "Tell me, how did your movie studio get tangled up with Stardust?"

He looked away, as though he were considering a lie, then thought better of it when he realized the truth was less damaging. "That's the kid's business, not mine. Stardust makes the girls happier, more willing to put on a show, that's all."

"Right. Finally, where did you and Marsha Black go after making movies on Washington Boulevard the other night?"

Again, he considered making something up. Probably an old habit of his from the days of sitting in court and lying left and right to make sure whatever sucker had been brought in on a charge was put away. But he hadn't done anything wrong, he felt, so he spit out the truth. "She wanted to get high again," he said. "I didn't have any dust and the kid had closed up shop. She got pissy and made me pull over on Keystone, around 72nd. When I stopped the car, she jumped out and ran away."

"I got pictures of you putting Stardust in Marsha Black's arm. Remember that, should you decide to tell McElroy or anyone else about our conversation." I left him there to think about it. By the time I got to my car and turned around, he was gone. No doubt he was running late for another adventure in independent cinema.

Acting like a bigger man than I was took a lot of energy. I could smell daylight approaching. Whiskey was in order. I made like a demon for the nearest convenience store.

12

Around noon I started the painful process of rolling out of bed. With my eyes half open, I reached for a cigar and the bottle. I walked to the chair behind my desk and sat down. I must have had some energy when I got home that morning because I had gone so far as to take my slacks off. I looked at my boxers. I couldn't remember the last time I changed them.

In the middle of this profound investigation, something I sensed from the corner of my eye made my skin crawl. I looked around. Ghosts had bothered me in my office before, perhaps they had returned. The childish part of me considered that maybe it was the spirit of Lorraine, visiting me to cause a heart attack and finish the job she took on the night she tried to shoot me.

Then I looked out my window, at the apartment across the street. The vacant room was no longer for rent, apparently. It wasn't a family running about, screaming at one another and desperately finding excuses to leave, no, nothing ordinary like that. In the center of the apartment, which was still otherwise empty, a gaunt white man in a black suit sat on a wooden chair. He wore mirrored sunglasses reflecting the mid-day sun that failed to prevent my realizing he was staring right at me.

I turned my chair completely around, so I could look back at the son of a bitch and relax. He didn't flinch. Whoever he was, he was good. I suppose I should have been creeped out by the whole affair, but you do what I do long enough and just about anything seems normal. Eventually, I got tired of playing his game and decided to leave.

It had been almost a week since I showered. I strolled into my bathroom, shut the door and cleared the tub. Before resting the strips of negatives on the sink, I took a quick look at them, thinking maybe there was a clue I had missed. No such luck. I shoved the chemicals and developing lamp by the door and proceeded with the arduous task of washing myself.

As I got dressed, I relented not having done my laundry to coincide with bathing. My brown suit didn't smell too bad, but every pair of boxers I had looked unfit, even for me. I decided to go without underwear. It brought back memories of my days as a photographer for the *Indiana Daily Student*, down in Bloomington. My pictures won awards left and right and artsy-fartsy gals who thought a great intellect was packaged with a kind heart would take me up on the most outrageous propositions. I never wore underwear then because extra clothes only slowed things down.

I put on a brown coat that went with the suit, wrapped a red tie around my neck, stuffed Lorraine into my left pocket, my Apaches in the right, and carried the whiskey under my arm.

I drove downtown to the public library on Meridian, down the road from the Veteran's Memorial. They had computers hooked up to the Internet. I was curious to see the kid's handy work on the Indy Friends site. It had also been a while since I'd suckered a woman into my bed. I needed a thrill.

Bums slept on the stairs leading to the library. One of them sat up and asked, "Excuse me, sir, can you spare some change?"

I looked at him, directed his attention to the way I was dressed and said, "Do I look like I can spare some change?"

He showed me his middle finger. I could respect that.

The main lobby looked like an old dance hall. Marble steps led to stacks on either side of the long ends of the room. A lady with her hair wrapped so tight it looked as if her skin might tear her face off pointed, without saying anything, toward the left staircase when I inquired as to where the computers were.

The library had decided that all modern propaganda should be put in the same place. The Internet access was available in the periodicals room. The walls were occupied by shelves of magazines. In the center was a runway of rectangular tables. Each one had four monitors and keyboards hooked up to a PC in the middle. Most of them were taken. I found an empty computer toward the far end, across the aisles from the *National Review* and *National Enquirer*.

When I sat down, I realized I was surrounded by college kids. They were making their lives easier by using the Internet to do their research for them. The girl next to me, a pretty little number with a wool shirt and clean jeans, held her nose and looked at me as though I were a Catholic who had just wandered into a Klan rally.

"How's it going, cookie?" I knew damn well she would be offended by the way I addressed her. That was the point.

She forced herself to look back at her monitor.

I typed "Indy Friends" into the search engine. A hundred web pages came back, but the first one was the only site I was interested in. I clicked on it and prepared to wait.

The title page loaded up at the speed of light. There was money behind the project, more than the kind Jerome McElroy and an intern from Daisy could muster up. The sponsorship banner at the top of the screen was a scrolling ad for some psychobabble outfit called Manifesto Destination.

"Feeling blue?" the ad asked. "Sleep too much? Sleep too little? Addicted to drugs or alcohol? We can help, make the call..."

The number flashed, and then the name of the organization, once more, Manifesto Destination. Why advertise that sort of nonsense on a porn site? I wondered. Anybody making proper use of porno shouldn't have problems sleeping.

There were two choices at the main menu. One arrow directed viewers toward the movie gallery. "See Local Gals Get Down and Dirty!" a button underneath the arrow suggested.

The other option was apparently a chance to meet and "date" one of these fine Indy gals. My friend SpaceDog failed to mention that aspect of the site. I clicked on the arrow and waited.

The next page featured two vertical rows of photos of young women with their stage names underneath them. I directed my pointer toward a brunette calling herself Amber.

Amber's lair was a layout of still shots taken from her film. She was unusually attractive for a call girl. She had short brown hair with faint red streaks. Her dark, brown eyes were almond shaped. Her lips, in every photo, arched in a manner suggesting she wasn't thrilled with the direction her life had taken.

At the bottom of the page was a phone number next to a list of rates. For three hundred dollars, it appeared, I could enjoy her company for a few hours. What that probably meant was a bit of small talk and then a quick one. No doubt as quick as possible, as far as she would be concerned.

I scribbled her number on a piece of paper provided by the library to record information, I suspected, other than the kind I was taking down. I stuffed the note in my pocket, clicked the "Home" button at the top of the browser, then turned and saw that my friend next door was gawking at me. When our eyes met she shook her head in a slow, "shame-shame" manner. I licked my lips and winked.

"Keep your snout in your own trough, cupcake." I got up and left before she could hand me her lawyer's business card.

13

I stopped off at the Eagle's Nest, a rotating bar on top of the downtown Hyatt. With the prospect of old man Black's money, I decided, I would drink in style every now and then. I sat in a booth by the window and watched the city crawl around me at a turtle's pace.

A waiter approached after helping a pair of fossils decide what brand of tea they should enjoy before requesting two plates of crackers. "Hi there," he said in that fake cheerful voice service people create in effort to earn a minor buck. "Can I get you a drink before you order?"

"I'm ordering right now," I said. "Whiskey and water. Jim Beam. Don't skimp on the juice. Three fingers, you dig?"

He looked confused, thought of asking me what the hell I meant, then closed his mouth and went back to the kitchen.

As the joint rolled past the west side of town, I noticed an unusual amount of police and emergency activity by the White River Recreation Center, a picnic area near the zoo. Two fire trucks, an ambulance, and a dozen police cars were parked on the bank of the river, sirens still turning. A news van from the local CBS station arrived. When they tried to get past the yellow ribbons placed around the scene, a couple of boys in blue pushed the brave journalists backwards.

I got a sick feeling in my stomach. The waiter returned with my drink. Suddenly, I was the sap in need of some crackers.

"I'd like a slice of wheat bread, toasted," I told him. "No butter, just toast."

He looked at me funny, again, like he had never heard of someone ordering plain, dry toast.

I worked on my drink. The kid hadn't listened to me. It was all water and a spit of booze. I could hit any number of dives downtown where you had to carry a gun just to be safe and get a drink built a hundred times better. Rich folks were always finding ways to rip you off.

The waiter brought me my toast. "Anything else?" he asked. He probably expected me to order squid with a side of sauerkraut.

I shook my head. By the time I finished eating the bread, my table had circled around once more to the west. I could see, just barely, a body being pulled from the river. The other three networks arrived, though none had any better luck getting past the yellow tape.

I left a twenty on the table. If my bill was any more than that I would gladly have gone back to the kitchen and thrown up the lousy drink they insulted me with.

14

It was close to four, Felicia should have been off work by then. If she was straight with me, she'd be at home, working on her newspaper.

Before driving to the Sanders Housing Projects, I stopped at a phone booth. For many reasons, some of which I don't care to discuss here, I felt the urge to talk to Amber. I dialed what turned out to be her pager, then entered the number I was calling from and waited.

A few minutes later, the phone rang. I let it ring twice. "Hello?"

"Somebody page me?" The voice on the other end was impatient. I could tell she was chewing gum and in the background I heard a young child trying to talk to her at the same time.

"Is this Amber?"

"Sure, what do you want?" Amber hadn't been schooled in the politics of customer service, apparently. Then again, she was in a business where she pretty much held all the cards and wasn't by any means required to give a damn about me.

"I'd like to spend some time with you," I said. "I saw you on the Internet and, I hate to admit it, but I got a crush on you just looking at your picture." I did my best to come off like a genuine goof.

"Gee, thanks." She sounded as enthusiastic as a heroin junky settling for aspirin. "When do you want to meet?"

"How about tonight?"

"I'm not supposed to see people the same day they call," she explained. "Angela likes to feel them out first."

I wanted to say I thought that was her job. "Who's Angela?"

"She runs the business." Amber, or whatever her real name was, sighed. "I'm free, though, so I guess I'll go ahead and do it. What time?"

"How about nine o'clock. Ramada. Downtown, on the circle."

"OK," she said. "Just wait for me in the lobby."

Before cruising over to Felicia's, I decided to take a look at the nonsense by the river. I drove west on Washington Street, toward the Hoosier Dome. The road curved at Victory Field, the baseball stadium across from the zoo. When I got to the approximate location of the action I witnessed from the Eagle's Nest, the area was quiet. There was only yellow tape. No vehicles, no cops, no medics.

I pulled to the side. There wasn't any legitimate parking, so I put my flashers on. Ducking underneath the tape, I strolled down the bank of the river.

About ten feet out into the water, there were four steel rods with red tape wrapped around the tips set up in a rectangle roughly large enough to hold a petite human being. I looked toward the sky, toward a God I had shunned since I was boy, and silently prayed it was nobody I was familiar with.

I climbed back up to the street. I got in my car and drove with clenched fists even *Charlie Parker With Strings* couldn't relax.

15

Felicia was home, working on her newspaper. When she let me in to her apartment she rushed right back to her office.

I nodded toward her son, who glanced up and screamed in acknowledgment. I walked into the office and looked over the paper as she had so far laid it out. Nice and big on the front page was a photo of Marsha Black taking dope in her arm. A headline ran across the top of the picture, "Daisy CEO's Daughter Caught in Porn and Drug Ring."

Felicia had her back to me. I grabbed her, turned her around, used my free hand to cup the bottom of her chin and tilt her head high enough to face me. "What the hell is going on, lover?"

She yanked herself free. "You wouldn't have gotten involved if I had told you everything."

"You could have tried half the truth, baby. You never know."

"Look," she said, resting a hand on her hip, "you don't understand how difficult it is to raise Tony, put out *Little Brother* and pay for this damn apartment."

"You got a tissue for my tears?"

She changed the subject. "Daisy Chemical is going to

own half this city if somebody doesn't check them."

I played along. "You think your little rag of poignant gossip is going to stop Leonard Black?"

"No, but it could generate enough interest to bring the mainstream media in on it."

"Right," I said, realizing it had been nearly an hour since my last drink. "Daisy just buys up property downtown like it's next to free, and you believe you're going to convince anyone with a fraction of sense more than you to join your crusade?"

"OK, OK." She threw her arms up, feigning surrender. "The truth is, this is my ticket out of this shithole. There's no way this issue of *Little Brother* won't get me work at a big time newspaper."

"So money's the answer to everything?" I took out an Apache, remembered there was a child in the other room and put the cigar back in my pocket. I didn't believe a word of it. No matter how hard I tried to look Felicia in the eye and get her to drop the truth, she was bent on feeding me another line. It occurred to me then that she was probably in cahoots with somebody else. "All right, baby," I said. I headed for her front door. "You let me know how things work out."

She sighed, realized that revealed more than she had wanted, and then folded her arms over her chest. "Thanks."

I opened the door to the hallway and turned around. "For what?" Maybe I liked listening to her talk, even if every word she said was a lie.

"For helping me."

I grunted and left.

Once upon a time Felicia had been, in my eyes, the perfect woman. We went dancing and watched movies and talked and got along swell. I was still in love with Lorraine though, and it took all I could muster to keep the relationship with Felicia from moving beyond platonic. Lorraine ditched me, temporarily, for some guy she claimed had better morals than me. I gave in to Felicia's advances and the two of us made music I'll never forget.

Then Lorraine returned, used her body to remind me why every man in the known universe would kill to be with her, and I ditched Felicia. I was twenty-nine-years-old. The bottle had only begun to make me smart. At least, that's the excuse I use to get to sleep at night.

Long after Lorraine tried to shoot me, Felicia and I stayed close. She never let me in as much as she had when I led her to believe we might become a permanent item. In the end, I was just another man who betrayed her, like her ex-husband, a white guy who helped her create Tony and then vanished when the doctors explained to him what "autism" meant.

Now she had tangled me up in the type of political situation bigger men than myself perished in more often than not. I was scared for her and myself. More for me, actually, and that meant one thing:

It was time to drink.

16

I sat in the Red Key, just off 52nd and College. It was an old joint, owned and operated by the same people since the 1950s. They played swing music just loud enough to hear without it getting in the way of conversation or, in my case, thinking.

While watching a television over the bar, I enjoyed three very well made whiskey and waters. On the tube, a local newscast reported the day's tragedies and then offered advice on what to name your new pet. Midway through, hidden between one of the four different weather reports and sports highlights, they mentioned a body had been found in White River, though they claimed it was unidentified at that point.

I tried like hell to believe otherwise, but I knew it was Marsha Black. First thing tomorrow morning, I told myself, cash Leo's check. If it turned out to be his little princess that went swimming in the river, he'd probably tell me to forget about the case. My dreams of retiring early and working full time on digging my grave with a bottle of booze were in danger of being put on hold. Again.

17

When I got to the Ramada downtown, Amber was waiting for me. She was dressed in a yellow shirt that cut off just above her belly button. A pair of faded blue jeans hugged her hips. Her hair was down and she looked even more gorgeous in person.

"Amber?"

She stood, grabbed, and hugged me. She pressed her body as close to mine as possible. Any questions I had about the sort of dates Indy Friends had to offer vanished. "Let's get a room," she whispered.

The Ramada was a renovated bank building, constructed in the 1920s by one of the many German architects who built Indianapolis from a small town to a big town with a handful of skyscrapers. The night clerk sat at a desk behind a teller window. To the right of the massive lobby was a row of old-fashioned caged-elevators.

I threw a fifty on the counter.

"It's seventy-five a night. I'll have to see some ID." The clerk was a hefty young man, no older than twenty. He punctuated every single word, begging me to question his authority so he could call the cops and have me thrown out.

Instead, I tossed another fifty across the counter.

"Make something up. Keep the change. Leave us the hell alone and I'll hit you again when I leave."

Money was the best medicine. He put the two bills in the drawer, made change for himself, then yanked down a skeleton key off a board behind him. "Room 108," he said.

After stuffing the key in my pocket, I put my arm around my expensive date and walked her to the elevators. "So," I said, trying to ease into a three-hundred-dollar interrogation, "you're Amber, the one and only, eh?"

"That's right." She put on her nice gal mask, now that the possibility of earning some bread was more solid than a voice on the phone.

The elevator arrived. I pulled the cage back and we stepped in. I shut both sets of doors and punched our floor. The ancient monster rumbled up a flight.

The hallway was made up like a fancy hotel. New burgundy carpet had been laid down and large potted plants were placed in between every other room. We turned the corner to a corridor decorated no different. 108 was halfway down.

The room itself was worth about twenty dollars. A shabby bed sat in the middle, flanked on both sides by small tables, each carrying a lamp. A card table by the window had a radio on top of it that looked as old as the building itself. Two folding chairs were propped, unopened, against the window. The neon sign blazing down the side of the joint made the room glow red.

I took my jacket off and turned the radio on. It had a circular dial making it difficult to tune. After a minute I found my station. They were playing Chet Baker. Perfect, I thought, then turned around and saw that Amber had taken off her top and was sitting on the bed in her bra and pants smoking a cigarette.

"What you in the mood for?" She looked at me with the same kind of eyes Marsha had—dark, scared, and begging for someone to slap them back into reality.

"How about we talk?"

"No chit-chat," she said. "Let's take care of business." She had obviously been doing this for a while. Women who worked in the sex racket eventually grew tired of pretending to care about their clients any more than they had to.

"OK." I strolled around the table and took her arms in my hands. "Let's dance."

"Are you serious?" She looked like she might laugh.

"Yeah." I hoisted her off the bed and wrapped her arms around my neck. "I never went to the prom, see, so I got a thing about dancing to good jazz."

She shrugged. "Never heard that one before."

"Never been asked to dance?"

"Nope."

You couldn't have fit a playing card between us. Each turn she pressed herself against me to remind me she was there strictly for business. I was ready for a romp, but I needed information first.

"So how long have you been with Indy Friends?"

She glanced at me, trying to decide whether or not I could be trusted. "Few years."

"Tell me about yourself." I tried to sound casual.

"What do you want to know?"

"Is Amber your real name?"

She shook her head.

"How old are you?"

"Twenty-two."

There was no polite way to maneuver around my next question. "Why do you do it?"

She grabbed my pants and loosened my belt.

"Just a minute, sweetheart." I pulled her back, ran my hands along her hips and under her arms. "I'm just curious. I've never done this sort of thing before."

She must have figured she wasn't going to be able to call it a night until she played ball. "I got pregnant when I was eighteen, started dancing, and one thing led to another." The trip down memory lane drew some bitter notes, judging by the tone of her voice. "If that bastard had stayed with me," she trailed off, decided she didn't want to give anything else away.

Instead of throwing her on the bed, like every fiber outside my conscience wanted, I buried her nose in my shoulder. Something about her took me back. She was wearing Fendi. I had only encountered one other woman under the age of forty who wore it:

Lorraine.

As Chet Baker gave way to Duke Ellington and Johnny Hodges, Amber inched us to the edge of the bed. Once she had me turned in the right direction, she pushed me over. I was out of whiskey for the moment so I gave in and we continued our dance in the closest possible way.

18

We lay in bed for two hours. Amber rested on her stomach and I ran my fingers along her back. The woman had managed to make me happy.

"If you could do anything else," I asked her, "to raise your boy and all, would you?"

She mumbled into the bed sheets. "I guess."

"I'd like to see you again," I told her.

"Sure." She rolled over and looked out the window. "I got to get home." She sat up and gathered her clothes.

"That little waltz we did brought some peace to my mind." For reasons I still don't understand, I said, "Genuine happiness, do you know what that is?"

As she put her pants on, she said, "My little boy will never be poor. I'm cool as long as he's happy."

"That's fine. What about you?"

She stopped.

"Look around. People shove each other out of the way to get wherever they're going. Nobody respects nobody. Money folks take advantage of the rest of us, and we shoot and rob each other to make ends meet. We plug into televisions, dope. Me? I drink like a fish. But a true moment, between two human beings, well that's pretty damn rare."

She finished dressing, lit a cigarette and exhaled in my face. "It was just a fuck, Elmore." Then she excused herself and floated out the door.

I laid back and tried to predict what other lousy tricks life had yet to play on me.

19

A maid beat on the door at eight o'clock in the morning. She had no sympathy. I dressed and left the room. On my way out of the hotel, I caught sight of the headline on the *Indianapolis Star*: LEONARD BLACK'S DAUGHTER MURDERED.

Beneath the shocking announcement was a photo of the boys in blue pulling Marsha Black from the White River. One of the harder lessons a man learns as he grows older is that his worse intuitions are always accurate. Before doing anything else, I realized, I had to cash Leo's check.

There was an Indiana National Bank on Monument Circle, just west of the hotel. I walked through a crowd of suits and ties rushing to work where they would sit still for eight hours spilling ink on paper that, in any rational world, wouldn't mean a damn thing.

The bank had just opened. There was one person ahead of me in line. A tall blonde in a short skirt. I stared at her legs while I waited. I couldn't help smiling. The illusion I allowed myself in Amber's arms the night before worked like morphine on the soul.

Another blonde, this one a little older, called me to her window. I handed her the check, scribbled my name on the back and slid my driver's license across the counter.

She saw the amount, raised her eyebrows, sized me up and shook her head. "I don't think so."

"Don't think what?" She snapped me right out of my good mood. Worse, I could already tell I wasn't going to see a cent.

"I'll call Mr. Black." She walked away before I could respond.

I had one Apache left. I lit it. A security guard shuffled over. He looked like he might have a heart attack from all the joy his job brought him.

"Sir?" That always killed me, how some jackass who got beat up one time too many in high school called you 'sir' just before rubbing your face in a heap of dime store authority. "No smoking."

"You don't actually smoke cigars."

"You know what I mean." He tapped his foot. I could tell his threshold for patience had been tested.

"Here you go." I handed the cigar to him, letting it drop to the floor just before he could grab it.

As he knelt down to pick it up he said, through clenched teeth, "Thank you, sir."

Ms. Wonderful returned with my check. "Mr. Black said to void this. Says he doesn't need your services any-more." She ripped it up right in front of me. "For obvious reasons." She nodded toward a metal box outside on the sidewalk that had the morning's paper in it.

"Of course." I tipped an imaginary hat and left the teller and the security guard to discuss the finer points of nothing.

20

I went to the City Market. Among the fruit and vegetable pushers inside was a cheap shop selling pints of whiskey and packs of Apaches. I restocked on the necessities and headed back outside. My car was parked in a garage on Delaware. As I stumbled across the street, I got an inkling:

Margie Crumb might have some information worth more than a nickel. Even though we weren't cozy like the old days, we occasionally met for dinner and I'd test her resolve to be true to whatever chump she was currently calling her boyfriend. I changed course and made my way to the basement of the City-County Building.

Gray steps in a dimly lit stairwell bled into the concrete hallway leading to the morgue. Margie's place of business was divided into three rooms. The first was the examination area. Four tables supported dead folks awaiting their final medical check-up. A narrow room to the right served as an office for Margie and two other examiners. Beyond that was the ice box for the dead. Green tiles lined all three rooms and a yellow light generated a stale atmosphere one might imagine a doctor's office in hell looked like.

Margie was working on an overdose victim that had

been found early in the morning. She had cut the stomach open and was separating digested food when I entered.

"What's up?"

She smirked. "What do you want?"

"Wondered if you might know something about Marsha Black."

"I was on duty when they brought her in."

"Cause of death?"

"Why?"

"Paper says she was murdered."

Her eyes popped.

"That's right. Daddy's little princess was whacked. I figured maybe if I knew how, I might know why, possibly even, *who* did it."

She moved to the refrigerator. I followed her.

Since Ms. Black came from good financial stock, she had a spot close to the middle. Margie pulled out the slab Marsha's corpse occupied. The girl looked worse than I imagined. From the constricted state of her skin, I deduced she had been in the water for a good six hours before the cops found her.

"When they brought her in," Margie said, "they said it was a homicide. But I emptied her belly and found the residue of enough aspirin to kill five people."

"Aspirin?"

"That's right." She produced a file from her desk. "A young woman like this who can't get anything more reliable will usually down as much aspirin as she can. I've seen it a hundred times."

Her report read "Suicide." I grabbed my forehead.

"You OK?" She put her hand on my shoulder.

"Who's seen this?"

"Nobody, yet."

"I want you to tuck this away. Unless somebody asks for it, don't show it to anyone. The powers that be are content with the public considering it a murder."

"I can't do that."

I looked at her. The case was getting so damn twisted I wasn't sure I could explain it if I wanted to. "There's some really nasty weather coming over the hill. I'm going to keep an eye on you."

"What are you, my father?"

"You still live on Compton?"

She put the folder under her arm and shuffled her right foot from side to side.

21

I drove back up Delaware. My conversation with SpaceDog, it turned out, wasn't complete. When I got to his parent's house, nobody was home, not Mom, Dad, or Junior. I knocked on the door, then beat on it. No neighbors were out in their yards. I decided to break in.

The window I climbed through before was open. I dropped into the basement and noticed the barrels with Stardust in them were gone. Just in case SpaceDog was playing hooky and hiding in the next room, I tip-toed to the door and cracked it enough to drift in.

Junior wasn't there. His computer was humming. I sat down to have a look. His Internet access was restricted. I had no clue as to what sort of password a dork like him would use. Scanning the other programs he had, I spotted an address book.

There were three sections in his computerized black book. One was titled "Friends," another was called "Business," and the last was an abbreviation, "I.F."

The friends file seemed harmless enough. About ten different names, all guys with one exception. The business portion appeared to be colleagues from Daisy as well as Purdue University. The Indy Friends file had exactly three names in it: Jerome McElroy, Abe Miller, and a woman identified simply as Angela.

Angela.

It was time to give her a call. I picked up a phone sitting to the side of Aaron's computer and dialed the number he had listed for her. It rang twice.

"Indy Friends."

I hung up.

It was Felicia Hill.

22

I called Express Taxi and asked for Leonard Black. A woman informed me, with a voice more somber than necessary, "Mr. Black has taken some time off."

I found Leo's address in the phone book. He lived in a bungalow near Conner Prairie Farm, far north of anything I was familiar with. It took me an hour to drive there. When I passed 96th Street, a cheerful blue road sign announced, "Welcome to Carmel." As if to punctuate that sentiment, I was followed twice by local cops eager to beat on some city rat bringing the suburb's dirty side to light.

Leo's place was located at the far end of a beautiful drive through a forested area off 96th and Allisonville. The house itself was a replica of a small Chinese palace. It was white with red trim. A long, narrow porch attached it to the cobblestone driveway. When I pulled up to the walk leading to the front door, five goons stepped out to greet me.

"What the hell do you think you're doing?" The tallest and fattest of them appeared to be their leader.

"I need to speak with Leonard Black."

"You can make an appointment with his secretary."

"It's about his daughter."

They looked at each other for help. I wondered if the problem I presented them might make smoke come out of their ears.

"Wait right here."

The head goon disappeared inside. The other four stood with their hands behind their backs, glaring at me as though I had just tried to shoot the president of the United States.

A moment later, Leonard Black appeared, dressed in a gray suit. He was working on another Cuban.

"I told the lady at the bank our business was finished. I apologize, but as you may have heard, and if you're any kind of snoop worth a damn, you sure as hell should have, my little girl was killed."

I shrugged off the drones standing between us. "Can we speak privately?"

Leonard raised his right hand.

The goons retreated.

"Your daughter committed suicide."

For the second it took the news to seep into his fat head, the world stood still. "What the hell are you saying?"

"I talked with..." I realized I had messed up. "Trust me."

"Mr. Johnson," he said, "I know who my daughter was. The negatives I saw in your bathroom were nothing of a surprise. Marsha was a drug addict. She used Stardust. The folks she ran with, well, they were of a life lower than even you."

"I appreciate that."

He ignored me and continued. "Girls like Marsha are murdered all the time. Who knows what else she was involved with? Sooner or later she was bound to recognize the element she was associating with and either she was going to wise up, or get killed, or worse, thrown in jail."

"How is that worse?"

"Murder is a nice, tidy package for the media. For my sake, nobody with any decency will poke around for more dirt."

"Forgive me for saying so, but you don't sound so tore up."

"Marsha is not a blood relation, if you must know. My wife Sarah brought her into the marriage. We never got along when she was little. She had no respect for her mother. Frankly, I'm relieved that in a short amount of time, I will never lose sleep watching my wife pace back and forth wondering what the hell her daughter is doing at four in the morning."

I sighed, found an Apache in my pocket and lit it. "Mr. Black," I said, "regardless of what you want the good folks of Indianapolis to think about you, Marsha *did* commit suicide. Why do you suppose she would do that?"

"Why does anyone cash it in on their own accord? I believe the psychology business calls it 'depression.' For a better understanding of that, I would refer you to an organization I often donate money to called Manifesto Destination."

"What good can they do?"

"The people at Manifesto Destination recognize the unhappy lives so many are subjecting themselves to. Drug addicts, especially. Counselors who volunteer at Manifesto Destination lift these trodden spirits back to the surface."

I took a drag off the Apache and reached into my

jacket for a pint of Jim Beam that wasn't there. Before I could ask Mr. Black how Manifesto Destination was saving these lost souls, he answered with one word:

"Seraphim." Leonard Black shoved his Cuban back in his mouth. "Soon we will all be happy."

23

It was late. I figured I should stop in on Margie. I had other questions for her, like, what exactly Stardust might be doing to the brains of the twits who used it. She lived in Broad Ripple.

Margie's duplex was part of a housing community called The Estates. Maybe they were, in 1941. With Broad Ripple High School directly across the street, they were two-bit wanna-be condos for schmucks who made just enough money to fool themselves into believing they weren't poor. Each unit had a porch with large columns, adding to the illusion.

I parked in between a fire hydrant and a tow truck. The lights in Margie's house were on. When I got to her front door, I saw that the lock had been broken and the handle ripped off. My stomach turned. I did my best to ignore any ideas of what was waiting inside.

The door creaked like a small animal being tortured. I let the door mask the sound of my feet clomping through. Something was burning in the kitchen. I called out, "Margie?"

Her apartment, like all the others on the block, was arranged with a narrow hallway at the center of a living room on the right and a kitchen and dining room on the left. A stairwell in the middle led to the second floor where two bedrooms and a bathroom made the rent seem like a real deal.

There were pots on the stove boiling over. I crept into the kitchen and then grabbed my mouth to keep from throwing up the toast I had eaten the day before—

Margie was on her belly, on the floor. The back of her head had been peeled open. In her left palm was a .50 caliber hand gun. Whoever shot her left a note written in pretty, cursive handwriting. The gist was suicide.

I wasn't fooled.

Margie was right handed.

24

An old college buddy of mine, Charles Watts, taught chemistry at the IUPUI campus downtown. I drove to the science building off of Michigan Avenue. Maybe Chuck was there, maybe not. Time was running out and bodies piling up in a manner that made me uncomfortable, even with a fresh pint of whiskey in my jacket.

IUPUI was an odd hybrid of Indiana and Purdue University, a mix of literature and engineering degrees for the truly schizophrenic. The science building was part of a modern complex joining the library with the computer labs and the engineering hall. The four structures combined to form an "X," if you had the vantage point of a bird.

Chuck's office was on the third floor. I ran up the stairs, nearly knocking over students with books in their hands and the goofy, ignorant smile of youth pasted to their faces. Had I been in a better mood I might have apologized.

The halls in the science building were white, sterile, like a hospital. I wondered how anyone could possibly thrive in such a depressing environment. Before reaching Chuck's office, I had to catch my breath. I fumbled the bottle out of my coat, secured it and spun the lid off. I took a healthy swig. Two students, one male and one female, passed me with disapproving eyes. They would learn, I figured. As soon as they were out of the safe, naive confines of school, they would learn.

By the grace of whatever controlled fate and coincidence, Chuck was in his office grading papers. His door was open.

"Elmore Johnson! What the hell is up?"

I entered the office, a small number lined with bookshelves overflowing with texts revealing every chemical wonder known to Man thus far. There was a black vinyl chair by the door, no doubt intended for students. I sat in it. "Brother," I said, "I am in some serious trouble."

"What else is new?" Chuck laughed. Watching me step into one hassle after the next brought him endless amusement. He had chosen to marry and settle down and lead what some might call a normal existence. In rare moments, such as then, I envied his ability to keep his shoes clean.

Where would I start, and how much should I tell him? On a whim, I asked him about Stardust. "The creator told me it's a mix of ecstasy, crank and cocaine."

Chuck winced and drew back at the thought of those particular chemicals dropped in the same blood stream at the same time. "I'm sure it's a hell of a trip," he said.

"And?"

"It's three stimulants. Got to be bad on the heart. Most important, though, is the speed, no pun intended, the combo must work at depleting serotonin levels." He rubbed the beard that covered just his chin, a style he had worn since college. "In fact, I would venture to guess that it only takes very small amounts of that stuff to wipe out the brain's capacity to create serotonin altogether. I mean, we're talking a matter of days. The addition of cocaine guarantees the drug is addictive, maybe the most addictive yet."

I thought about it. "What happens to someone who can't produce serotonin?"

"We've seen it in crack addicts. They might kick the drug after ten or fifteen years of using it on a daily basis. Soon into sobriety, however, they suffer severe depresssion. About ninety-percent of the time, they commit suicide."

"Any way to repair the damage?"

"Not really." He looked out a small window by his desk. "Best you can do is supply artificial serotonin."

I did some math:

Seraphim.

25

It was early, but I wasn't sure what my next move was. I wondered if anyone had put me at Margie's around the time of her death. Maybe I'd get another visit from Jerome McElroy. I sure had a few things to discuss with him. My best move was to head back to my office, drink myself to sleep and snuggle up with Lorraine close enough for comfort.

Outside my apartment, I felt something was wrong. I pulled Lorraine from my pocket and held her ready. Kicking my door in, I jumped through, only to have the gun knocked out of my hand by a gorilla in a white lab coat. I was thrown to the ground and the same guy who attacked me shoved his foot on my face and held it to the ground. Two other men in lab coats jumped on my arms to keep me from moving.

I craned my head upwards and saw that the jackass I had a staring contest with the previous morning stood over me with a syringe in one hand and my camera in the other. He released the latch on the gate the film passed through to be exposed. My photo essay on the extra-curricular activities of cab 525 vanished.

"Sweet dreams," he said. His monotone voice sug-gested a lifetime of mastering a way to communicate without revealing any emotions. He leaned down, jabbed the needle in a vein in my hand and pumped my blood full of Stardust.

26

The first wave of Stardust felt as though someone had stuck fishing hooks into my skin, all over my body, and ripped them away simultaneously. The sensation of a million bugs crawling over me followed and for reasons completely chemical, I felt the urge to laugh for the next six hours.

I was never a fan of illegal drugs. My experience with Stardust reinforced my opinion that dope was for people who really, *really* hated themselves. I may not have enjoyed my life, but I loved *me*. Ask any woman I'd ever dated. Whether the events that followed took place in my mind or in the physical world or, possibly, both, I'll never know for sure.

My apartment melted and morphed into a stark room. I was dressed in a suit and tie my mother used to make me wear to church. She was there, so was my dad. Next to me was my brother Bill, who drowned when he was eight and I was thirteen. The first thought that ran through my mind was that I treated Bill like crap and the son of a bitch died before I could apologize.

Upon this revelation, I cried. Oh, I was still laughing on the outside, but that was just to show the world how tough I was. Being a real man and all, I held the tears in as long as possible. But the crying gag brewing inside was too powerful. My stomach heaved and under the impression of Stardust, it felt like waves crashing against my heart. When the waterworks started for real, the room filled up like a fish tank.

Bill drowned in the canal running along Broad Ripple Avenue and Westfield. It had steep banks and was rumored to be well over twenty feet deep.

One day, Bill was riding his bicycle along a dirt path on the side of the canal. He passed through an area called Rocky Ripple. Bill heard the sound of kittens, crying for help. He hopped off of his red Schwinn Stingray, a sturdy bike he inherited from me when I graduated to a ten speed. Crawling down the bank, he saw that someone had dumped a garbage bag filled with baby Calicos into the canal.

Understand, Bill was the tallest kid in his class. He was a late bloomer, meaning he didn't walk until he was a year and a half, and he didn't talk until he was four. Mom and dad put him in classes for the learning disabled, as the education folk liked to call it, and in addition to being terrorized by his older brother, Bill was subsequently picked on at school. Mind you, he could have pulverized just about anyone his age—he had monstrous hands and, thanks to me, learned how to fight with a determination most only wish they possessed. But he never struck anyone who didn't deserve it and, more valiantly, if he saw someone mistreating somebody weaker, he would rush to the scene and beat the high holy shit out of the aggressor.

Be the bully who bullied the bully. That was the only thing I taught him. It was one of the few ideas my dad passed on to me.

And so this little boy with a heart bigger than the world itself jumped into the canal, unaware that one should know how to swim before diving into a large body of water, and reached out to pull those kittens back to shore. I had tried for over twenty years to ignore thinking about what went through his head as the water dragged him under. Did he ever stop to consider himself, I wondered, or was the thought of helpless goddamned animals taking up all the room in his suffocating brain?

I floated there, in a pool of my own tears. People used Stardust for fun, I remembered. How the hell was that even possible?

The sun broke through the top of whatever hallucinogenic island I was stranded on. I swam toward the light and surfaced through the drain of a sink in a boy's restroom at Broad Ripple High School. The bastards who shot me up with dope had failed to remove my good suit, so I took every precaution as I crawled out to keep dirt from smudging my clothes.

Maybe I was a fool. Perhaps Bill's death inspired me, unconsciously, to be a better person. As I walked through the filthy bathroom, I noticed a ruckus by the urinals. Three Fountain Square thugs were putting the squeeze on a lanky dork named Matt. Matt was an effeminate boy with spiked hair. He wore a Ramones T-shirt, jeans, and combat boots. He probably believed that dressing like a freak would ward off teenaged Neanderthals.

"Give us your boots, too," one of the thugs said.

Before I could help the kid, I walked in and did the job for me. Me, that is, from 1980. I pulled out a switchblade and threatened to cut up anybody who made a wrong move.

As the scenario unfolded, I remembered the actual

incident, and how the fruity, wanna-be punk rocker ran for his life while the three Southsiders ganged up on me and beat my face bloody. They handed me my switchblade back and suggested I not tell the principal if I didn't want them to talk about the knife. It was a fair deal. It inspired me to seek other ways to compel justice.

My dad bought me a camera the year before he died. "Son," he told me, "this world is controlled by ink and mirrors. What happens in real life doesn't mean a damn thing if it ain't down on paper." Then he handed me the camera and said, "Nothing tells a better story, though, than a picture."

I began shooting everything I could—food fights in the cafeteria, fist fights in the hallways. Then I took a few pictures of asbestos hanging from an open tile in the ceiling of the school. The teacher who ran the newspaper found them especially interesting when three of her colleagues dropped dead from lung cancer and not a one of them smoked cigarettes.

The school vanished and I was back in the white room. I couldn't make out any visible borders. From what seemed like a mile away, a person appeared. A woman. She floated toward me and I relaxed for the first time since venturing into Stardust's grip.

As she got closer, I saw she was wearing a black, silk, full-bodied skirt. She was a brunette with lovely eyes and a sway to her walk that told me she didn't have a fear in the world. Only one woman was that ignorant of her own frailty.

"Hello Elmore." Her voice dripped through my ears like honey and molasses eased over warm flapjacks in the middle of winter. The walls breathed in and out, mimicking my own breath. Colors bled like paints dropped from the sky and Lorraine Monroe leaned forward to kiss me.

We were eighteen. We were in Bloomington, Indiana, strolling along railroad tracks to a pass cut through a quarry of limestone. Lorraine told me her life story.

"Monroe is my mother's name" she said. "I had it legally changed because my father, well, he and I really, *really* don't get along." She rubbed her arms. I put mine around her and pulled her in close. "The earliest memory I have," she continued, "is of my two dogs I had when we lived on a farm. I fed them store-bought chow every day. They seemed well behaved. I trusted them, you know?" She stopped and stared at me. Her eyes disappeared, replaced by pale light, and her voice transformed, like a cassette played too slow. "One day I looked out the window and watched them tear a tiny rabbit from limb to limb. The worst part, however, was seeing them fight over who got to eat what part of the corpse."

I reached out for her, but she vanished. As I tried stepping off the tracks, I was hit by a train I couldn't see. The impact knocked me up and backwards. I never felt the ground. Instead, I found myself swimming in a pool of stars.

Lorraine's voice, coming from thin air, addressed me:

"What are you going to do with your life?"

I shrugged, causing a rip in the fabric of space. The sun poured through and I fell flat on my face in a dorm room on the Indiana University campus. The sound of two kids fumbling around, trying to have sex, directed my attention to a bed underneath a poster of *The Lord of the Rings*. My face turned red.

From the looks of things on the bed, I had a lot to be embarrassed about. The woman, who I assumed was

Lorraine, was on top of me. When she leaned back, allowing me to get a better look at her, I saw that she was every woman I had been with whenever Lorraine would have a psychotic episode and disappear. Her face transformed, as she struggled to get as much pleasure out of the moment as I did, from Hanna, a cheerleader who lived in the dorm across the street, to Julia, a girl who had the ill fortune of occupying the room directly below mine.

I grabbed my head. I couldn't believe what a pig I had been. The woman on top transformed one last time into Lorraine. When she saw how ashamed I was, her head turned, slowly, three hundred and sixty-degrees. I tried to stop her head from rotating, but it only sped up until it became a drill. She lowered it into my chest and I watched my rib cage shatter and my heart explode. I passed out.

When I opened my eyes, I was in my apartment on 38th Street. Everything was quiet. I looked down and saw that I was once more intact. There was no furniture, no refrigerator, just my camera and a bottle of Jim Beam.

The sound of a phone ringing scraped my ears. I looked up and saw that I had no ceiling, just a view of outer space. "Mr. Johnson?" a voice said. "We'd like to bring you out to Los Angeles for an interview. Alan Feldman has expressed interest in hiring you as a set photographer."

I grabbed my camera and a plane ticket. They dissolved in my hands. The bottle was my only possession. I picked it up, unscrewed the lid, tilted my head back and found myself on a bed in the middle of an endless dirt field. Lorraine was on top of me again. We were making love, a little more skillfully than in the previous memory, but she wasn't smiling. Tears formed at the corners of her eyes. I lifted her hands up. Her blood warmed my arms. She had slit her wrists.

I rolled off the bed, wondering how the hell I could get her help out in the middle of nowhere, and found myself in a church. I stood up and walked down the center aisle. At the altar was a coffin. I didn't want to know who was in it, but the red carpet had become a conveyor belt, and the pews on either side gave way to a void. I peered past the walkway carrying me toward the altar and saw pitch black.

Finally, I put my hands over my eyes as I was transported right up to the coffin. My fingers vanished and I gave in and glanced down. My mother had a smile on her face, convinced she had done the best she could. I wished her well, put my hand on her forehead and then ducked as it began to rain diet pills the size of footballs.

I dropped to the floor and realized I was in the corridor of Central State, an institution for the mentally scarred. How many times had I visited Lorraine there? Jim Beam had seen to it that I would never have an accurate count.

The walls slid past me and stopped at a particular door. There was a small window toward the top. I looked in and saw her, walking back and forth. Scars from the tubes they had put in her at St. Joseph's hospital hadn't healed.

"Lorraine?"

Everything went dark. I was in bed in my apartment on 38th Street. The light from one star shone down as Lorraine emerged from nowhere, once more on top of me.

"I've found a way to solve all our problems." She

kissed me and pointed a .38 at my head. "Don't worry. I'll be right behind you."

There was a gunshot. Then there was nothing. No lights, no darkness, no thoughts, no memories.

Nothing.

27

I opened my eyes with the sort of effort it must have taken to carry a stone across the desert in Egypt, back when they built the pyramids. A light glared down so harsh it felt as though it were burning a tunnel to my brain. Little else seemed to work. My arms wouldn't move, neither would my legs. The drug had worn off. I gathered in as much as my limited vision would allow. Someone had put me in a white room with no windows. Then I realized I wasn't alone. Turning my head, resisting the urge to scream from the pain it caused, I saw the gaunt man who had been so kind as to provide me with the dope seated in a metal chair at the foot of the bed.

"Welcome back to reality, Mr. Johnson." He had no clue how lucky he was that I couldn't move.

"Who..." Each word took careful concentration to deliver, "the...hell...are...you?.."

The jolly old bastard smiled. "I am Dr. Thomas Burden, and I am fascinated by you, Elmore Johnson. You told me your life story in eighteen hours. I was particularly impressed with the way you seemed to come to an understanding about the way you treated, ah, what was her name.., Lorraine?"

Speaking of Lorraine, I thought, where's a pistol

when you need one?

Dr. Burden continued. "The overwhelming pain you're experiencing is called withdrawal. I'm sure you're familiar with the idea. Stardust, a nasty little composition I stumbled upon quite by accident, takes the psychologically addictive qualities of crack cocaine and couples them with hallucinatory grandeur that forces the body to fiercely crave the drug, even after the first dose. A campaign is already under way in your brain to destroy the natural neurological manufacturing of serotonin."

I knew all that. I wanted to hear the saintly chemist give it to me in his words.

"You have but two options now. Your body would like nothing more than another dose of Stardust. It's convinced. There's nothing you can do to stop it from thinking those eighteen hours represent the best that life can get." He pulled a capsule out of his pocket and held it over my nose. "The wiser choice is Seraphim. It will artificially reproduce serotonin and you will feel no urge to go back to Stardust."

The energy to tell him where to stick his drugs was nowhere to be found. I pursed my lips, held them together as tight as possible, but Dr. Burden was much stronger at that point. He forced the drug into my mouth and clamped it shut. The pill made its way to my throat and then my stomach. The effort required to complete that routine knocked me out once more.

28

The next time I woke up I felt great. When I tried to get off the bed, however, I saw that I had been strapped to it. I couldn't figure out why. Life was a rose with petals you could pick and then watch grow back. There was no concept of time threatening to wipe out everything I ever tried to accomplish.

So I laid there with a smile on my face. If they must keep me here like this, I thought, why not put a window in the wall so that I may look outside and see the sun? Nothing sounded quite as wonderful as birds chirping, dogs barking, or the infectious laughter of children.

"Hello!?!" I was hungry. It was nothing to get upset over, though.

A nurse walked in. She had summer blue eyes and country blonde hair. She introduced herself as Heather. "What's the problem, Mr. Johnson?"

"No problem," I said. I grinned like an infant being tickled by the Easter Bunny. "Just wondering if I could get some food."

"Dinner is served at eight." She tilted her head and smiled. Her teeth were white as snow and perfect as a pure cloud in a high-August sky. "We've been feeding you intravenously. Now that you're awake and calm, I'll be happy to bring a fork and spoon and regular meal for you tonight." She added, "Anything else?"

I could feel tears of joy welling in my eyes. "I would really like a window. I want to see the sun shine, see if it competes with the warmth you exude."

Heather giggled. She licked her lips and then smacked herself in the head. "Um..." She put her finger on her chin to help her think. "I have an idea!"

She shuffled out of the room. I wasn't worried in the least. I knew she had my every interest at heart. The world, for that matter, cared about and loved me more than I deserved. But even that was okay, because I had nothing but the same to offer right back.

After an amount of time too small to note, Heather returned with a box of crayons. "I'm no carpenter," she said. The bright light in the room reflected off the whites of her eyes. "I think I can make you a sunny day without all that fuss anyway."

I studied her the way beasts sized up prey. There was a voice inside me suggesting what I really wanted was to rip a path through Heather's uniform and panty hose and hump her like a starved dog on a wild rabbit. But that's exactly what I would have been—a wild animal. If my hands had been free I would have slapped myself for harboring such aggressive impulses.

Heather knelt by a spot on the wall directly in my line of vision. She fashioned a window frame with a brown crayon. As she craned forward to draw the top, I could see much farther up her skirt than I'm sure she would have preferred. Despite my newfound ability to ward off the desires I felt watching her, there was one part of my body I could not control. It announced its presence in a manner that made the restraints more uncomfortable than usual.

When the good nurse drew the cross in the middle of the window frame, she dropped the crayon and said, "Fiddle-sticks!"

"What's the matter?" I asked.

"I think my drawing of the sun will not be scientifically accurate." She turned around. Her eyes focused on my naughty part which, she could tell, had focused on her.

"Mr. Johnson!" She drew her head back and gasped. "I think it's time for more Seraphim." She marched out of the room.

I could feel tears coming on. The last thing I wanted to do was hurt Heather's, or anyone else's, feelings.

She came back and stuffed a pill in my mouth and forced me to chase it with water from a Dixie cup she practically crammed into my face. As the drug went down, my body relaxed. All of it.

"Very good." She went back to drawing my window. The sun was interrupted by the cross in the frame, but I could tell what it was and felt the love Heather put into it. What I really wanted was to give her a friendly kiss on the cheek. She must have read my mind, because she added two doodles that were obviously birds. With a green crayon she drew a palm tree. I could hear the ocean, tapping at the shore just outside.

"Heather," I asked her, "could you tell me something?"

She nodded, gathering up her crayons and listening to me at the same time.

"Where am I?"

She brushed her hand at me in a girly, "oh stop it" manner. "Silly! You're at Manifesto Destination. We saved your life."

* * *

Heather continued to care for me. She fed me oatmeal every day and night. She propped my head against her shoulder and read stories to me such as the tale of Tit and Tat:

"Tit," she read, "woke up one morning to discover there was only one waffle left in the refrigerator. She looked around, saw that her brother Tat wasn't paying attention, and put the waffle in the toaster. Before the waffle finished cooking, Tat wandered into the kitchen looking for a waffle he could eat. He saw the empty box in the trash can, noticed his sister standing by the toaster, and confronted her. 'Tit,' said Tat, 'you know I enjoy waffles as well, why have you tried to eat the last one without consulting me?' Well, Tit would have none of that! She responded, 'What makes you think you are entitled to it?' The waffle popped out of the toaster and the two of them looked at it, then at each other. They realized they had entered into a *conflict*." Heather always paused at that word, making sure I was still paying attention. "Conflicts lead to hurt feelings. 'I have an idea,' said Tat, 'So do I,' said Tit, and each offered a hand to pull the waffle out and rip it in half. By the time they finished eating their shares, they had forgotten all about the *conflict*."

When I asked if I could have some music to go with my window, Heather brought a tape player in and put on a looping cassette of two songs by Don Ho. Whenever I told her I could see her dancing in a grass skirt and offering me a lei, she gave me another pill.

Once a day two gentlemen who looked as though they might have played that awful, aggressive game called football, untied my restraints and allowed me to walk around my room in a circle for what they claimed was an hour. It seemed much longer to me, but I suspected that was because I preferred lying down and staring at the sun.

Dr. Thomas Burden visited me and we had a terrific talk.

"Elmore, you aren't upset with me, are you?" He sat in a folding chair near the foot of my bed.

"Why would I be?" I realized he was blocking my view of the sun. "Oh, I get it. If you would be so kind as to move a scratch or two to your right, I would have absolutely no reason to dislike you, Dr. Burden."

The doctor looked over his shoulder, saw that he was indeed obstructing my view of the great outdoors. "Good grief, man," he said. "How could I have been so thoughtless?"

"Think nothing of it." I tried waving my hand, but it was still tied down.

Dr. Burden moved his chair and then proceeded with the issues on his mind. "I wonder, Elmore, if you are ready to work, to become a part of society again."

"Why wouldn't I be?" The question was absurd—not that I was in any position to judge the validity of another person's curiosity.

"I can allow Heather to remove the restraints?"

I nodded. I felt like a puppy being set loose in the front yard.

Dr. Burden left and returned with Heather. "Nurse, I think our boy Elmore is ready to take his first steps in the new world."

Heather bent over me. She was wearing a scent that made me think of the girls at the Magic Carpet. As she untied the restraints on my arms, I felt the urge to put my hands all over her body. Maybe I just wanted another pill.

She climbed onto the bed to loosen the leather around my ankle closest to the wall. I was certain she didn't want me looking up her skirt and seeing that her stockings stopped at her thighs and, for whatever reason, she hadn't worn any panties.

"Mr. Johnson," she said, "looks like you're due for some ethical persuasion, yes?"

She was right.

"I think so," I said.

Heather smirked, which confused me. She retrieved another dose of Seraphim. "Would you like to take it yourself?" She held out the pill and a cup of water.

I took the water and cradled the capsule in my hand. For the first time, I noticed a smiley face imprinted on the drug. Looking at the happy pill made me feel wonderful. I popped it into my mouth, chased it and handed the Dixie cup back to Heather.

Dr. Burden spoke up again. "I'd like you to attend a DA meeting tonight and tomorrow we will start the process of assimilating you into society with a job."

"DA?"

"Dependents Anonymous. We've combined all drug and alcohol addictions into the category of Dependence."

"I was, a..."

"Dependent. First on alcohol, and then you became hooked, as so many unfortunate souls, on Stardust."

I couldn't believe it. Had I not seen the commercials on television warning me about drugs? I wanted to give

Dr. Burden a great big hug for rescuing me from myself.

"Heather will escort you to the meeting after supper."

Heather patted me on the head like a dog.

That night, Heather brought me a bowl of oatmeal and allowed me to feed myself. It didn't seem as gratifying as having her do it, but I knew thinking like that led me to ideas that society considered bad.

After dinner, Heather and I walked through the hallway together. It was white, like everything else, and filled with rooms just like mine. Happy and sad people occupied each one, learning how to feel once more. If I could have offered a hug to the ones who were still struggling, you bet I would have! Heather tugged my shirt, though, insisting we move faster.

We got to a sterling silver elevator and took it to a lower level. There were no numbers on the buttons indicating the floors. I suppose withholding information like that confused anyone resisting happiness. But I knew the difference between Heaven and Earth, and after Heather bent over to push one of the lower buttons, the first thought that ran through my mind was, "going down."

When the doors opened, we traveled another hallway. This corridor differed from the others, however, as it had red carpeting and pictures of flowers on the walls. We walked past a series of glassed-in offices to a gymnasium.

In the center of the gym a circle had been fashioned from folding chairs and people sitting in them. They glowed with as much joy as I did. Heather directed me to an empty seat.

A tall white man with a blond afro stood up, looked at me and asked, "Who has joined our circle?"

I peered over both shoulders, pointed at myself to make sure I was the one he was addressing, and responded. "My name is Elmore."

The congregation said, in unison, "Hi Elmore!"

I nodded down the line, trying to make eye contact with everybody there.

"Why don't you tell us about yourself?" The man with the afro held his hand out the way a poor homeless soul on the street might ask for change.

I shrugged. "What do you want to know?"

A woman in a jumpsuit two sizes too small said, "What was your poison, sweetie?"

I had to think about what she meant. Had I been taking poison as well? Then it hit me, "Oh," I said. "I was addicted to alcohol and...Stardust, I guess."

There was a collective murmur. Folks nodded their heads and offered sympathetic looks. One gentleman wearing shoes with the toes worn out stepped over and gave me a hug. "Welcome home, brother," he said.

"Thank you." I sat back down. Something disturbed me. I couldn't figure out what or why. I had taken my Seraphim on schedule. Yet, I was feeling *conflict*.

As the evening progressed, I listened to the others talk about how miserable their lives had been before Seraphim saved them. A factor I believe called *intuition* suggested I keep the doubting voice in my head to myself. I had come so far, the last thing I felt I needed was to be strapped back down and subjected to the joys of Don Ho and Heather's window.

29

"Time to go to work, Elmore." Dr. Burden sounded almost as happy as I was. I wanted to ask him if he took Seraphim.

I was escorted to my new job in a black limousine. I had never traveled in such luxury and I would be a dirty liar if I said I didn't enjoy every second.

"Don't get used to this," Dr. Burden said. "I thought we'd let you experience your first day on the job with a little class."

In the back of my mind, I wanted to suggest that some sort of drink would be a better way to celebrate. I dismissed the thought as left-over misery from the days before I was saved.

We drove through downtown Indianapolis, past many people walking to and from their jobs. Some of them seemed happy. Most of them looked sad, even angry. A few struck me as downright homicidal.

"You see what I see?" Dr. Burden was gazing out his tinted window.

"Misery?" It felt great to be on the same wavelength with another human being.

"Bingo."

We passed Monument Circle and turned onto a street

near the football stadium where people hurt each other for the enjoyment of the sour masses.

The limo pulled into a lot near the Magic Carpet, a seedy establishment where men treated women like sex objects. The very thought of such a business in my hometown made me ill.

Once again, Dr. Burden was thinking just the same as me. He nodded toward the den of sin and said, "Don't worry, son. We'll eliminate that filth in due time."

As we made our way to the building I would be working in, I felt again as though something were wrong. My heart sped up and I got the impression that the claws of demons were marching their decayed fingers along the rim off my skull. I reached into my pocket and found my bottle of Seraphim. I grabbed a capsule and swallowed it.

"First day jitters?" Dr. Burden put his arm around me in a chummy manner. "You'll do great!"

The limo stopped in front of a white, art-deco building. It was the Vonnegut Lofts. A giant near the street read: DAISY CHEMICAL—NO TRESPASSING

Dr. Burden waved to a security guard. The gentlemen with a badge and a gun opened a barbed-wire gate and directed us through.

Thirteen rows of Daisies graced both sides of the cobblestone walk leading to the front door. It smelled like a thousand summers. I thought of little children, enjoying their time away from school, dancing in a grassy field.

Glass doors with red trim, twice my height, opened automatically and we stepped through. Inside, there was a long corridor with massive steel doors along either wall. The floor was concrete and the smell of daisies gave way to a powdery scent I recognized.

Halfway down the hallway, an inlet led to a room with

a plaque by the door reading: EMPLOYEE LOUNGE

Couches lined the short ends of the room while the far wall was covered by a colony of lockers, some padded shut, some open. A bar supporting white lab coats on hangers stretched from one end to the other. In between the couches on each side was a restroom for the different sexes.

"Take a coat." Dr. Burden instructed. "Change in the bathroom, then meet me back out here."

The bathroom was a marvel of symmetry. Along the left wall were urinals, the right, stalls, and two sinks at each end reminding me to wash my hands after making potty. I took off the scrubs I had been dressed in at Manifesto Destination and put on the lab coat. When I passed myself in a mirror hanging over one of the sinks, I peeked at my reflection. The white coat made me look very smart, but I had trouble maintaining eye contact with myself. I hurried out before I could think about it anymore than I had to—

Dr. Burden had been joined by a skinny, younger man in a white coat. He stepped forward and offered a hand.

"Elmore," said Dr. Burden, "this is Dana. He'll be your supervisor. He'll tell you all you need to know."

"Pleased to meet you," I said as I shook his hand.

"Likewise." Dana had blonde hair that was almost white and his eyebrows dipped outwards when he spoke. He looked sad, but it was an illusion. I could almost smell the Seraphim on him. Inside, he must have been a bundle of rainbows.

"This is goodbye, for now, Elmore," said Dr. Burden. "I've enjoyed our time together." He took a deep breath. It seemed to me he was holding back tears. I considered offering him a dose of Seraphim. He patted me on my back and then hurried off before I had the chance. When he was down the hall, well away from the employee lounge, I heard him break into laughter. I concluded he probably had his own prescription.

"Good old Dr. Burden," Dana said.

"Indeed."

"Shall we go to work?" He unfolded his arm like a flight attendant pointing me to a seat on a plane.

"Lead the way."

We walked further down the corridor and arrived at a large metal door. Instead of opening outwards, Dana had to slide it left in order to allow us access to the room.

Inside was a hollowed out warehouse with a series of rectangular counter tops. In the center of each was a pile of yellow dust. Workers sat around the perimeter scooping up the substance and balancing it on a tiny scale in front of them. They adjusted the amount to a specific weight and then put it in a plastic baggie, tied it up, and placed it in a duffle bag at their feet.

Several workers pushed large wooden carts around the room. When somebody at a table filled a duffle bag, they would exchange it for an empty one and start the process over.

As I entered, a cart filled with duffle bags was pushed past me, through the door and down the hallway I had just been in.

Dana pointed to an empty work station near the back. "How's that look?"

"Perfect."

As we made our way to the other side, Dana filled me in on some important details. "You're paid by direct deposit. Daisy takes care of all your bills, in fact. The only thing you need outside of rent is food and transportation. At the end of each week, Daisy provides you with vouchers good at Preston Safeway and Shell gas stations."

Could it be possible, I wondered, that Daisy had taken all the stress out of life?

As if he could read my mind, Dana said, "Ain't it grand?"

We arrived at my work station. Dana directed me to pull the empty chair out and sit in it. He picked up an aluminum scoop, dipped it into the large pile of yellow dust in the center of the table and dumped it onto a balance beam scale at my elbow. "You want to weigh out one ounce." After adjusting the substance to the desired amount, he opened a cupboard by my station and produced a box of sandwich baggies and tie-on clips. "You do this until your duffle is filled, then start over. Easy, isn't it?"

"Quite," I said. I was overwhelmed with the joy of having a job that required no thought.

For eight hours I stuffed baggies with yellow dust. Time flew. All I did was sit there and repeat the same task, over and over again. My recollection of life before Seraphim was vague, but I remembered struggling from day to day to make ends meet. I recalled refusing to get a normal job. I couldn't figure out what made me think that was any plan for happiness.

When it was time to go, a whistle sounded and my co-workers and I marched out in a disciplined manner to the lounge. We took turns dressing in our street clothes.

Someone replaced my scrubs from Manifesto Destination with my black suit from the days before salvation. It was cleaned and pressed. As I put it on in the bathroom, I realized I would have to send someone a "Thank You" card.

Outside the plant, my Towne Car was sitting in the parking lot. A security guard stood next to it with a smile on his face. When I got close enough, he handed me the keys.

"Congratulations on your first day, Mr. Johnson."

The sky was gray. But that was only if you didn't have the right attitude. All I saw was the sun, playing peek-a-boo to humor me.

I got in my car and drove to my apartment on 38th Street. At each traffic light, I observed my neighbors on the road. It was painfully obvious who was on Seraphim and who wasn't. Angry drivers clenched their steering wheels. When I tried to make eye contact with them they sneered. Some called me names I would never repeat in public. The blessed, however, sat back, obviously relaxed. They didn't mind waiting in a traffic jam. They nodded and smiled when I glanced in their direction. We knew we possessed a special secret. The most amazing thing about Seraphim was that, once revealed, it was a secret that begged to be shared with others.

30

My apartment had been cleaned while I was away. I took my jacket off and sat down at my desk. I thought I felt eyes on my back. I no longer minded. Turning my chair around, I looked at the apartment across the street from my window. It was empty. I imagined a time when a family would live there. I could make out their forms— Dad, Mom, Brother, Sister, a dog and a cat, all gathered around a dining room table eating and expressing to each other how much love they felt. But that was the future. Possibly even my own, I reminded myself.

I looked at my desk and pulled out the flat drawer. My .38 had a note taped to it. It was written in pretty cursive, the kind only a woman could craft:

You don't need this anymore!

I agreed. I pulled out the top of the larger drawers. My camera, lenses, and film were neatly arranged next to another note in the same writing that read:

This equipment is useless to a happy man!

The memo was absolutely correct. I slammed the

drawer shut with enough confidence to tear down a building, not that I would ever do something so aggressive and destructive.

"*But you did just slam that drawer,*" I whispered. "Shut up!" I had no idea where all that hostility came from. It was time take a pill. I was far enough along to recognize when my "secondary emotions," as Heather called them, got the best of me. I walked over to the bed, picked up my jacket and retrieved my bottle of Seraphim from the left pocket.

I took a pill out, popped it into my mouth and realized I had nothing to wash it down with. I scrambled to the refrigerator and found it had been cleaned and emptied. Not even a drop of water or ice. I ran into the bathroom. Everything had been stacked in an orderly manner. All my developing chemicals and lamps were piled in the bathtub with another note written in the same handwriting as the ones in the desk:

You certainly have no use for this, do you?

I turned the faucet in the sink. Nothing came out. Taped to the cracked mirror I normally avoided looking in was a letter, this one signed by my landlord. It explained that the water would be turned off for twenty-four hours as of, apparently, that day. The Seraphim was dissolving on my tongue. I gave up.

In the bottom filing drawer in my desk, a brand new bottle of Jim Beam rested with a red bow tied around the neck and one final note:

You're too strong to go here, aren't you?

Of course I am, I thought, I'll just wash the Seraphim down and no one will know. I opened the bottle and chased the pill.

As soon as the whiskey and Seraphim hit my stomach, I felt a rumble, as though an Earthquake were passing through Indianapolis. I had an urge to lie down. When I moved to my bed, I collapsed to the floor.

31

I had no clue what time or day it was. My head felt like someone had dropped an anvil on it, like in a cartoon, from the top of the Friendly Insurance building, the tallest skyscraper in Indianapolis. As I sat up, the room spun.

Somebody had taken me for a ride, a serious ride, and I wasn't happy about a goddamn thing. On my desk, a bottle of Jim Beam, tipped to the side and half empty, called my name.

I, Elmore Johnson, stood up and drank half a fifth of whiskey in one epic swig. The room slowed down. The walls found their proper places between the floor and ceiling. And the memories of the manure I had been dragged through rained down and painted my face furious red.

I was still dressed, basically, and only smelled half bad. Putting on my jacket, I reached into the flat drawer in my desk, pulled out Lorraine and left.

It was time for this bully to bully the goddamn bullies.

32

It was dark outside, meaning most of the cops and suits and ties at the City-County Building had gone home for the night. I would be able to move through the halls relatively safe of being discovered by eyes I didn't want spotting me just then.

I parked in a lot across the street from the side door, the most efficient path to the stairs. A couple of uniforms stood on the steps outside, drinking coffee and laughing at stories about you and me getting worked over for no good reason.

They didn't notice me. They were too busy with their java and fables of Constitutional Destruction.

The night desk was vacant. To conserve energy, half the lights were turned off. This allowed me to glide among the shadows to the stairwell.

In the basement, the only glow came from the morgue. I entered and found a coroner I had never met before.

"May I help you?" He was a little man, couldn't have weighed more than one-twenty. He had to look up, real high up, just to address me.

I pulled enough of Lorraine out to let him see that cooperating was his best wager. "You're going to do everything I tell you, understand?"

A puddle formed around his ankles. "Sure, sure."

"Margie Crumb. You worked with her?"

"Yes." He put his hands up.

"Don't do that." I knew better. If whatever fat ass night watchman was paying attention to the surveillance cameras, he'd come storming down there to play hero. "Who did the autopsy?"

"Um, I did." He looked down.

"Let me see your report."

"That's classified."

I shoved the barrel of Lorraine into his belly. "Show me the file or they'll be writing one on you."

I marched him to the office with the records. He pulled out a thin Manila folder with Margie's name on it and handed it to me. The genius had typed "Suicide" as cause of death.

"Sure," I said. "People are always shooting themselves in the back of the head. Especially women."

Einstein Jr. seemed confused.

"Women who snuff themselves rarely do it with a pistol. Margie most definitely wouldn't kill herself that way. She liked things tidy. A suicide she authored would reflect that."

"I wrote what I was told to."

According to the coroner's report, the investigating officer was Jerome McElroy.

I got a notion—"You know where the file on Marsha Black is?"

He nodded.

"Get it."

He dug deeper in the cabinet and produced another razor thin folder.

The cause of death space had been covered with liquid

paper and the word "Homicide" was written over Margie's determination of suicide.

"Well, well," I said. "Tit for tat."

The coroner rubbed the bridge of his nose. "Mister, you don't make any sense at all."

I put Lorraine back in my jacket. "This conversation never happened. You tell anybody, I'm the least of your worries. You just go right ahead calling murder suicide and suicide murder, you got it?"

"OK." He knew the best way to get rid of me was to agree with whatever I said.

"They find out you showed me these files, they'll kill you too."

That made him stop. He squinted at me through round spectacles with the dumbest eyes I'd ever encountered. The city'll employ anyone, I remembered. Once upon a time they even hired me.

33

Jerome McElroy lived, like most of IPD, in Beech Grove. Beech Grove was south of downtown. The general income was nice, but the residents were what "sophisticated" city folks referred to as "rednecks." Jerome blended in just fine.

His house was similar to every other joint on the block. It was a compact two story aluminum number with white paint hiding how cheap it really was. The whole neighborhood reminded me of *Leave It to Beaver* with a dash of Pabst Blue Ribbon and NASCAR. Cop cars lined both sides of the street. I had to park a minor walk away.

When I got to McElroy's place, I peered into the window closest to the door. Jerome was eating dinner with his wife, a make-up junky smoking Kool cigarettes while she ate and watched a talk show on a small black-and-white television propped by her plate. She washed her food down with Night Train. She drank directly from the bottle. My kind of woman. She couldn't have been much older than myself or Jerome. Damned if she didn't look a day over sixty.

Mrs. McElroy was seated next to her only son. I had never met him but he looked, at five or six, like he was destined to be just as upstanding and ethical as his dad.

He wore a pro-wrestling T-shirt with the slogan "God Hates You!" scrawled in sloppy letters across the back. His hair was spiked and every thirty seconds he scooped up some loose corn on his plate and flicked it at one of two dogs lying underneath the table.

Jerome's face was buried in a copy of *Neon Lights*, a local publication directing gentlemen to the best strip clubs in town. The cover was graced by a picture of a national porn star named Ann Tense. According to a headline under her mug, she was going to show off her talents at an area chain of bars in the coming month.

It was a cozy scene. I knocked on the door.

I heard his wife say, "Just who the hell would that be?"

Jerome answered the door. Before he could react, I called on Lorraine to inspire compliance.

"Step outside, buddy. We need to talk."

He looked over his shoulder and said to his family, "No worries."

The loving wife and son weren't concerned in the least.

"Johnson, you realize stupidity and nerve are the same thing, don't you?" He did his best imitation of a cowboy in a Hollywood western.

I tried to sound casual. It seemed the best route to some straight answers. "You and I have a lot in common."

He chuckled at that and spit over the side of the iron railing leading to his door. "Sure we do."

"Both of us have chosen paths in life most folks wouldn't readily consider what polite society calls 'acceptable,' yet we move forward, like tanks, without a care for anyone else."

"Don't make me out to be a scumbag like yourself, Johnson."

I laughed. "I can see why you'd think so little of me. I sold out you and your brothers on the force. But I was never a part of your club anyway, so I'm not too broke up about it." I searched my coat for an Apache. I had forgotten to pick some up. "Neither, apparently, are you too concerned with the heat *Little Brother* brought when they printed my pictures of you and the ladies on Washington Street."

"What does that…"

"You just expanded and moved, didn't you? Instead of hookers on Washington Street, you got dates for rent on the Internet."

He stood still. He broke the silence with a profound, "So? What you going to do about it?"

"How's Felicia mixed up in this?"

"I don't know what you're talking…"

"Give it a rest." I aimed Lorraine higher, between his eyes. "I called up the all-purpose hotline. My dear friend Felicia answered. I guess she's going by Angela when she works that particular job."

Jerome turned his head from side to side, made sure nobody was hanging out on their porch, looking in on the possibility of spreading some dirt around the donut shop. "Got a minute?" He opened the door and stepped inside, then held it for me to walk through.

His house smelled like shit, literally. I suspected the dogs were allowed to do their business wherever they pleased. We walked through a small room with a plastic-covered couch and television set in the middle and a box of broken GI Joe toys in the corner. There were bookshelves along the back wall—empty, save a few stacks of *Hustler* magazine mixed in with *People*.

We marched through the kitchen, which was actually

larger than the living room for reasons that meant nothing to me. His crumpled up wife gave me the once-over.

"Honey," Jerome said, not even facing her, "this here's a police photographer. We're going to have a look at something in the cellar." Then he stopped. "Oh," he said to me, "Elmore, this is my wife, Katie, my son Jerome Jr., and my dogs, Moe and Larry. Curly died last year. The cancer, they said."

Before I could acknowledge everyone I had just met, Jerome directed me to a small door. We stepped through and descended a brittle set of stairs. Rain and floods had probably softened and then weakened them. I held on to an equally unstable banister running alongside the wall.

The basement smelled worse. There were piles of dog shit, some old and petrified, some warm and new, all over the concrete floor. Jerome turned on a bulb hanging from the ceiling to reveal an impressive computer system. He sat down and clicked a mouse on the keyboard and navigated his way through a menu of files.

"Allow me to introduce you to the oldest movie in the Indy Gal archives." He tapped the mouse once more and a screen within the monitor emerged. "This was made just before you and Felicia Hill blew the whistle on us."

The camera zoomed in on a dark-skinned woman getting molested from every conceivable angle. Even though the lighting was bad, I could make out the anguished face of Felicia, doing her best to feign excitement. There was no way a piece of dirt like me could ever judge anything anyone else had ever done, but I found it difficult to rationalize why Felicia would hide something like that from me.

"When you and the little lady busted up the ring, we

114

found this in her house, an old sixteen millimeter reel she shot when she was dancing at the Magic Carpet." It was obvious he enjoyed pulling the plug on any remaining saintly ideas I had of Felicia.

"She worked at the Magic Carpet?"

"That's right, snoop. After her newspaper put the finger on us for dealing in the smut business, we thought it only fair to suggest she not point at us lest she face the three digits aimed right back at her."

"I don't get it."

"When was the last time Felicia's paper went after the police department?"

"You tell me."

"The Washington Street story. 1994, Elmore. Five years ago."

Scratching my head, still fuzzy from all the crap the good folks at Daisy Chemical had dumped into it, I searched for a counter to his claim. He was telling the truth, though. Felicia went after liquor store chains, churches taking money from grandma and grandpa. Until wrapping me up in the fine mess I was unraveling, she had taken no further shots at the City-County Building.

"So who has the original?" I nodded toward the computer screen. An image of Felicia was frozen in an expression that could easily be confused with pain.

"I tell you that, we don't hold the cards on Ms. Hill no more."

I smacked him across the face with the butt of Lorraine. "You looking to donate an early pension to your widowed wife and kid?"

"You wouldn't shoot a cop, Johnson. You only shoot women."

I squeezed the trigger and let a bullet destroy the screen on McElroy's computer monitor. Glass and sparks flew at his face. He put a hand over his eyes and stuck an arm out toward me to block any further slugs.

The basement door flew open and Katie jumped down half the stairs. "Baby!" she cried.

Jerome glanced at me, then addressed his beautiful wife. "It's all right, honey."

She looked at me as though I were some kind of monster. McElroy must have had her firmly planted in the dark.

"Do as I say." He snapped his fingers at her.

Katie stood on the steps for another minute, looking back and forth between me and her husband. She sighed. She probably assumed we were engaged in some violent pissing contest that only men understood. She wasn't that far from the truth.

When she was gone, Jerome threw some cards on the table.

"Abe," he said. He stared at a petrified dog turd on the floor.

"The Magic Carpet?"

"That's right."

I refrained from asking him about the autopsies. It seemed the very subject had disastrous consequences on one's mortality. I wanted to wait until I had the entire deck and everyone knew I was dealing.

"Sorry about the monitor," I said.

"I'll just get a new one from work." He moved to the stairs.

"Don't do anything heroic." I raised Lorraine once more.

He climbed the steps and, like a regular pal, showed

me to the front door without any static. It was only a matter of time, I figured, before officer friendly figured out a way to help me commit suicide.

34

I drove north, toward the Magic Carpet. The Seraphim had robbed me of the ability to negotiate my emotions. It made the act of thinking difficult as feelings of rage and the desire for vengeance kept creeping into the equations brewing in my head.

But I was too old to act on emotions. A younger man might get violent. Since the death of Lorraine, however, I discovered that the best way to settle conflicts was, in simple terms, finesse.

For instance, it took patience to properly make love to a woman. This lesson I learned after years of fumbling around that led to insults and attacks on my ego. Another example was the way I drove. With one hand on the top of the wheel, I leaned back and let the road move beneath me. And that was how I would resolve the mess Felicia had gotten the both of us into.

Business was good in the smut shack. Next door, the lights at the old Vonnegut Loft were still on. Semi-trucks lined up at the front of the building.

I pulled my car into the lot by the post office. Using a telephoto lens, I zoomed in. Carts of duffle bags were loaded onto the trucks. I watched one get filled to its capacity and then rumble out of the gates. There were a dozen eighteen-wheelers left on the lot.

Where were they taking the good doctor's dope? I wondered.

My first priority was getting the film. I kept close to the post office, so as not to draw any attention from across the street.

Inside the Magic Carpet, the stage was filled with every girl working that night. It was what the management called a *Red Light Special*. All the gals got up there at the same time and stripped and strutted, emptying the pockets of any man dumb enough to think he was gaining something by having twenty dancers each con a buck from his wallet in the space of a three minute rock and roll song. Genius, I called it.

Abe Miller sat in a round booth in the corner opposite the couch area. He had two flunkies on either side of him. A blonde with fake tits bigger than her head crawled on the table.

I strolled over, put my hand on Lorraine and sat down to Abe's left. His goons gave me a glance and dismissed me as nothing to worry about.

"We need to talk," I said over the music.

Abe raised his hand. His eyes were focused on the blonde on the table. "I'm auditioning a dancer right now. Come back tomorrow."

Suddenly, finesse didn't seem all that attractive to me. I grabbed the blonde's shoulders and slid her into the lap of the thug sitting next to me. The table was covered with drinks and tip money. I threw it to the side.

"Do I have your attention now?"

Abe shook his head.

The bouncer, a three-hundred pound moron with the words "Mr. Sensitive" written across his T-shirt, stomped over. I showed him Lorraine.

Mr. Sensitive put his hands up. Luckily, most of the folks in the bar were busy stuffing dollars at the stage. Even the DJ didn't notice the ruckus.

I walked into the space where the table had been and spoke as loud as I could without shouting. "You got moving pictures of Felicia Hill. I want the original, wherever it is."

Abe shrugged. "No idea what you're talking about."

The crony without a girl in his lap reached for a gun. I smashed the bottom of my right shoe into his nose. He spent the rest of his energy keeping his face together.

"We don't have the original," Abe said. "Once McElroy copied it onto his computer, we gave it back to Felicia."

He wasn't any more nervous than he should have been with a .38 pointed at his belly. I assumed he told me the truth. I backed away. Near the entrance, I stuffed Lorraine into my pocket. As soon as I heard the sounds of traffic outside, I busted through the doors and ran like hell for my car.

When I got to the post office, I glanced back. The flunkies were standing outside the club, smoking cigarettes. They didn't look like they were in the mood to chase after me.

My attention turned to another truck rumbling out of the gates at the Vonnegut Lofts. There were ten more on the lot and the carts of duffle bags kept moving. Judging from what I had seen earlier, they could have filled a hundred semis if they wanted.

I got in my car and waited. The trucks were headed

south. They might have been going to the corporate office by Madison Avenue. But I had seen the rate at which the dope was moving from Daisy to the taxi cabs to the streets. Surely they didn't need that much for one day, or even one week. The operation I witnessed at the Vonnegut Lofts had to have a larger purpose.

When the next truck was loaded and ready to go, I started my engine and followed it down Illinois Street. It rumbled up the I-65 on-ramp and headed north. Either it was taking Stardust to the good people of Shepherd, Indiana, or, more than likely, it was going all the way to Chicago.

I drove behind the truck for an hour. When it reached Lafayette and kept going, I pulled a u-turn and sped back to Indianapolis. I assumed the Stardust was headed for Chitown. The cops at the Steak 'n Shake had been right—the drug was going to spread across the country like a virus.

And Daisy, no doubt, would be ready and willing to solve each city's Stardust problem with a fresh batch of Seraphim.

I listened to *Charlie Parker With Strings* on the ride back. Coasting by the plains and farms, beneath a star-filled sky unmolested by city lights, I got nostalgic. I remembered things being a lot freer when I was a teenager. Folks who talk about "the good old days" are usually masking their fear of mortality, their painful yearn to be young again. Thinking about how Daisy was poised to spread its filth throughout the nation, I couldn't help but wonder if life might have been a little bit better before corporations decided they had a right to run the whole goddamn world.

35

I picked up a fresh pack of Apaches and a pint of Jim Beam to help me sleep. The convenience store was still trying to sell yesterday's newspaper. The headline read: DAISY TARGETS MAGIC CARPET.

More importantly, the date read August 4th, which meant I had been in the sterile clutches of Manifesto Destination for over a month. The math wasn't adding up, though. I knew Felicia was tangled with Jerome, and he was working with the same organization taking money to keep the cabbies moving Stardust around the city. Had Felicia been involved with the plan to turn me into a brain-dead self-help sap?

36

My phone rang all morning. I was too tired to answer it. I knew it was some twit from Daisy wondering where the hell I was. My sleep went, aside from that, relatively uninterrupted until two in the afternoon.

There was a quiet tap at my door.

"*Who is it!?!*" I hoped that would scare whoever it was into coming back later.

Instead, a bright, anxious and overly-sweet voice answered. "It's Heather! May I come in?"

It took me a moment to remember. Heather, the nurse. The no-panty-wearing ultra-friendly blonde who should have counted her lucky stars Seraphim repressed the beast in me every time she leaned over and wiped oatmeal from my snout.

I got up, dressed only in boxers and one sock, and answered the door.

As soon as she saw my half-naked, hung-over condition, she clicked her tongue against the top of her cherry-red mouth. "Oh, Mister..." She shook her head. "You're not taking care of yourself."

I stepped aside. Watching her thighs shift as she entered the apartment, I imagined sinking my teeth into her skin. "I know," I said, "I need you to hold my hand,

123

among other things."

She toted a large white bag to match her nurse's uni-form. I assumed she brought me some Seraphim, just in case I had forgotten how to turn my mind to mush on my own.

"You look damn good." I spoke in my Big Bad Wolf voice that would have settled all doubts between me and a grown woman in any other situation.

Heather glared at me. Her eyes skipped down my bloated belly to my crotch. "Have you taken your medi-cation?"

I slammed the door and locked it. "Not yet." I jerked toward her.

She backed into my desk, nearly spilled over it. Resting her palms on the edge, she crossed her legs and dropped half the syrup in her voice. "Dana reported you as absent without calling in. That's a serious infraction."

"Can it, baby." I planted myself in front of her, close enough to make her smell just how wretched my breath could get.

She struggled to appear cool and at ease. "What are we gonna do with you?"

"Intensive care, nurse. That would be the best plan of action." My eyes rolled like deep-treaded wheels up and down her body.

She tried to slide around me, maybe to make a break for the door. When she moved, I clawed straight up her thigh. The young lady still refused to wear panties. She feigned surprise. We both knew better at that point.

"What's your game, sweetheart?"

The nurse blushed, angled for the window. This time I let her go.

"When you start out," she said, staring at the empty

apartment across the street, "you don't think of decisions as having any consequences. I wanted to be a doctor, but I grew up on the east side in a family of seven, the second youngest. The only way I could get money for school was dancing at the Magic Carpet." Her eyes narrowed, like she had tasted something bitter. "I settled on becoming a nurse. The money kept me going back, though, until I agreed to do a favor for one of the big shots from Daisy. The take on that was even better." She reached into her purse and pulled out a pack of Camel cigarettes. "Do you mind?" she asked as she lit a match.

"Not at all."

She took a drag, flicked her wrist to put out the match, threw it in the ashtray on my desk and went on with her biography. "I made the mistake of telling one of the clients, another pencil pusher from Daisy, that leading the double life of a nurse at Wishard Memorial and a date-for-hire with Indy Friends was making me depressed. He turned me on to Seraphim. Once I realized the whole thing was a scam, I threatened to quit. By that time I had made a private movie and they said they'd show it to my parents if I left."

I found a half-burnt Apache on my desk, fired it up and contributed to the smoke filling the room.

"I see you ignored my notes," she said. "Good."

"I'm torn to bits about your situation, baby. Truth be told, I'm only interested in finding out what the hell gave Dr. Burden the idea to try and convert me."

"He's crazy," she said. "One night he called on me, said a friend recommended me. We spent about twenty seconds having sex and then he made me lay in bed with him and tell him all about myself."

"You give him the same story you're running on me?"

"I'm not lying, if that's what you think."

"I ain't thinking, baby." I took a drag, exhaled as I spoke. "Just listening."

"Tom, Dr. Burden, offered me a job with Manifesto Destination. He even got the Magic Carpet off my back. Of course I took it."

"You're lying to someone." I stood next to her by the window, made eye contact through our reflections in the pane. "You're not taking Seraphim anymore. Yet, you have no problem turning on your smiley face."

"Dr. Burden insists you can't quit using it once you start. When I realized how much it altered the personalities of the people at the clinic, I went against his warning and stopped. So far it hasn't had any effects on me. I see you quit without much hassle."

I picked up my bottle of Jim Beam and took a swig. "I got the best dope in the world."

She smiled. "When we searched and cleaned this place, Tom, he was afraid you'd go back to drinking. I suggested we take the bottle, but he said it was important to see if Seraphim kept you from falling off the wagon."

"I'm still not getting where I fit into this picture." I sat down on my bed.

"You knew about Stardust. Tom worried that you'd figure out he was involved in its creation. He had to kill you or assimilate you. At least, that's what he told me."

"A little dramatic, don't you think?"

She faced me for the first time since I put my hand between her legs. "You have no idea what he thinks he can accomplish." Her face was cold. She was light years from the bimbo routine I had grown to know and lust after.

"One more thing," I said. I snuffed the Apache with a third left and placed it on the edge of my desk. "Do you like feeling the wind up your skirt, or is there a better reason you don't wear undies?"

She blushed. "Dr. Burden has a peculiar notion of overtime." She put her cigarette out and made for the door.

"What are you going to tell your boss?"

"The truth," she said, returning her voice to Nurse Happy. "You told me to suggest to him he take that job and shove it."

"And yourself?"

"I'll probably commit suicide."

Nurse Heather exited my room. I was broke up. Not by her story, just the fact that she left without giving me some "overtime." I put her down as "things to do" and got ready for the day.

37

I drove to Washington Boulevard to have a chat with Aaron Milton. No such luck. When I got there a yellow ribbon danced around his house. I sat in my car, in the parking lot at the Greek Church, and watched a body wheeled out on a stretcher. The paramedics shoved the corpse of SpaceDog2112 into an ambulance. As far away as I was, I could make out a wound in the back of his skull. Another "suicide."

I started the Towne Car up and drove like a demon to 25th and College. If anyone was going to wring Felicia's neck, it was going to be me.

38

Whether she was genuinely concerned or just a great comedienne, Felicia nearly dislocated my shoulder when I walked through her door. "Where the hell have you been?"

Tony sat on the floor with some toys. He was fixing up a date between a Tonka truck and a stuffed lion. The Tonka wasn't going for it.

"I was at Denny's," I said, "enjoying a nice hearty Daisy Slam Breakfast."

"What are you talking about?"

"I went to every Denny's in town. You know what they told me?"

"Big deal, I don't work there. That doesn't excuse your ducking me for a month."

"I apologize." I sat on her couch, a hand-me-down with duct tape patching up half a dozen rips. "I was busy having phone sex with a gal named Angela."

She folded her arms across her chest. "Want something to drink?"

"Whiskey and water'd be nice. Three fingers, baby. Don't skimp on the juice."

"All I have is water." She went into her kitchen, grabbed herself a bottle of beer and poured some city sludge into a glass for me. When she returned, she handed me the offensive liquid. "OK, I lied to you."

"I know that." I placed the glass of water on the floor. "I'm curious as to why."

Felicia sunk into the couch next to me. Her eyes crawled the ceiling. Maybe she was considering telling me the truth. Instead, she handed me another goddamn line.

"My mother," she said, "worked three jobs to raise me and my sisters. Both of them were darker, I mean way, way darker than me. At school, kids in my class asked if I was white. I cried to my mother and asked her why I didn't look like Kendra or Cherelle. When I was older, she told me she had an affair with Leonard Black, way back when he was mopping the floors at Daisy."

I gave away just how much I didn't believe her.

"It's true, jackass." She punched me in the ribs. "She didn't know he was going to become the CEO. When I was barely in high school, she died. She was forty-eight years old. Didn't smoke. Didn't gamble. Didn't screw around. Didn't eat shitty food. She just worked too damn hard."

"Get me a paper towel," I said. I grabbed her beer from her and took a swig. It wasn't whiskey, but I thought it might help wash down her story. "I smell some bullshit that needs to be wiped up."

She stood, leaned over me, and dropped a motherese tone on me. "I'm telling you the truth, Elmore. You could stop being an assumptive prick and give me the benefit…"

I took to my feet as well to remind her she was a foot shorter. "The benefit of what? You have me tag a girl who essentially works for you. You have me follow a taxi driver who also, in a business way, is related to you. Now you're going to tell me this was all to, what, get back at Leo Black?"

"I'm his *real* daughter," she said. "I've spent five years trying to clean up my image. When Tony was born, I had no choice, he needed constant medical care. Dancing was my only option."

"What about the movie?"

She turned away. "They showed you?"

"Yes ma'am."

"What can I say? It paid the heat bill for an entire winter. I destroyed the original. If I could, I'd track down every copy and make sure nobody ever saw it again."

"I think you've got a worldwide audience."

"The agreement was, I worked the scheduling for them and my movie was kept private."

Sometimes I wondered why I even tried getting the truth from women. The tooth pulling session with Felicia was giving me a headache. If I didn't get some whiskey soon, I thought, I might have to join the local suicide club.

She saw that I wasn't in the mood for any more boo-hoo stories. "You have to believe me," she said. "I just wanted Leo Black to help me out. I thought I could convince him with the pictures of the cab."

"Good luck getting those," I told her. "A gentleman named Tom Burden, you might have done business with him at one time or another, found it in his heart to destroy the roll of film I shot that day."

Tony screamed at the both of us. Felicia walked over, picked him up and rocked him on her hip.

"Doesn't matter. It was suggested that I quit publishing *Little Brother*."

"By whom?"

"Jerome. He didn't like the attention the Magic Carpet got when folks read about Marsha Black's performance art."

"How'd you get mixed up with Jerome?"

She sent a look my way that had all the impact of a .44 slug shot point blank between the eyes. "How do you think?"

I shrugged.

"You came to me, remember? 'Ms. Hill, I have some pictures you might consider interesting.' It didn't take much for them to find me, come up with the dirt they needed."

"So this is all my fault?" I made for the door.

"I know you haven't left here with the most reliable information in recent times." She offered me the same sweet, innocent eyes Heather showed for a month at Manifesto Destination. "Those days are over." She put her hands on my shoulders.

I grabbed her wrists. "I'm sick of getting the okie-doke from the one person I thought I could trust."

She struggled out of my grip and opened the door for me.

"Don't go anywhere unless it's absolutely necessary," I said. "Don't let anyone but me in, understand?"

It looked, for a moment so brief I almost didn't notice, as though Felicia were going to cry. The thought made me ill.

"Save the performance for Indy Friends," I said.

She slammed the door in my face.

39

I had a professor at Indiana University named Dwight Keller. He taught philosophy and believed, as I did, that fate was in charge and freewill was an illusion that kept us all from cashing ourselves in with a gun to the face or knife to the wrist. He once told me his take on the picture of a man walking through the forest and arriving at a fork in the road.

"If you pick up a stone," he explained, "close your eyes and throw it without aiming, the wind will direct it to the path you were intended to take. But, even if you think you decide to take the other road, supposedly to laugh at destiny, ultimately, your option will still be the result of a power we are simply not constructed to understand."

I only brought that up to explain how I ended up paying a visit to Dr. Thomas Burden.

It started around two in the afternoon. I ducked into the Red Lobster on Keystone and 38th for lunch and some booze. After ordering a large bowl of clam chowder and a plate of toast and two whiskey and waters, I noticed someone had left a copy of the *Indianapolis Star* on the table next to me. Newspapers didn't turn me on, otherwise I'd a given up the snoop racket a long time ago.

And that's what made my decision to pick the paper up so baffling. I flipped through the sports section. The Indianapolis Colts clamored for a new stadium. Our basketball team, the Pacers, tried to figure out how to work the books in the off-season to keep Deacon Rose, the famous point guard, from selling out to the New York Knickerbockers. It was fascinating stuff to keep your mind off of your miserable existence if you punched a clock and scrubbed dirt and oil from your hands after work every day.

The editorial page was filled with the usual right-wing hypocrisy about making government smaller while trying to ban flag burning and abortions. Some things never changed, I thought.

I read through the world section and then the local news. In a story less than two paragraphs long, on the very last page, a little bit of information changed my plans for the day. The headline was all I needed to see: SERAPHIM PATENT TO EXPIRE

I finished my meal, downed both drinks. The bartender, or whatever halfwit they had in the kitchen mixing up the death-fuel, completely skimped on the juice. When the waiter handed me my check, I refused to pay for them.

The manager brought me a bottle and asked me to demonstrate how to make a whiskey and water. I wrapped three fingers, the middle ones, around a glass and dumped Jim Beam in it until the liquid danced above the edge of the top finger. Then I splashed it with a hint of water.

"That's way too strong."

"Nonsense," I said. I downed it to prove it. Then I mixed up another one, offered it to the manager.

"Oh, not while I'm on the job." He shooed the drink away like it was poison.

"Fine," I said, and drank it. I suggested pouring another one, to ensure they understood how to make it, but the manager stopped me.

"I think we got it," he said.

At the far end of the parking lot was a phone booth. I stopped my Lincoln in front of it, dialed information and asked where Tom Burden lived. I was surprised when the operator told me. I figured he'd be unlisted, seeing as how he was about to become the richest man in Indianapolis.

40

Dr. Thomas Burden lived in a small red house in a middle-class neighborhood on the parameter of Broad Ripple. A screened-in porch covered the front of the joint. Tom was no fan of neatness, apparently, as he let the grass grow taller than my knees. Ivy trailed up and down the outside walls and at least a dozen trash bags littered his driveway. There was no car in the street. I assumed he was off saving souls.

I walked around the side. The back yard took up three times as much land as the house did. Dr. Burden had planted an assortment of daisies, tulips, and other pretty flowers I'd need an encyclopedia to identify. In the center was a stalk with a pod-like cap. A nasty little homemade barbed-wire fence circled it. I had seen it before, in documentaries on eastern lands we had gotten into futile wars with at one time or another. It was a fully matured poppy.

"Well, well," I said to myself. "Easy to be in a good mood when you got opium growing on your lawn."

The back door to Tom's house was open. I knocked on it twice. Then I shouted inside, "Dr. Burden?"

I held my nose as I entered the kitchen. Grocery bags lined the back wall. They were filled with potato and egg scraps. Some of them had turned to compost. A worse odor came from the stove, where Tom had found it fit to place four pots with water in them. It was rain water, I suspected, judging from the twigs and grass leaves floating on the top. Along the walls, stuffed heads of deer and beavers stared into oblivion.

The next room appeared to be the lonely doctor's dining area. A circular glass table sat in the middle with two chairs on opposite sides. The upper torso of a female mannequin occupied the seat closest to the only window. She wore a black, silk skirt. In the center of the table, a plastic baby doll had been propped on her ass. I couldn't help but smile. Dr. Burden was a sick son of a bitch. I understood why a man like him would find so much comfort in a drug like Seraphim.

To my right was a narrow, extremely small hallway leading to a bathroom on one end and, I presumed without checking, a bedroom on the other.

I was drawn to the front room. More hunting trophies hung on the wall. A stereo system rested in a glass display case on the side closest to the door. A couch and small television were in the middle and a fake fireplace graced the other wall. Above it was a rack cradling three Marlin shotguns.

There were two pictures resting on the stereo case. I picked them up. The first one was of Tom and a little girl, no older than five, captured in an embrace I perceived as too close for comfort. My deduction was pretty accurate because in the second picture, Tom stood next to a thirteen-year-old future bombshell who, it appeared, refused to be in the same shot lest they put air between them. Her arms were folded across her chest. I would recognize the peculiar pout her lips formed long after I was dead and buried...

Lorraine.

I heard the sound of a shell being loaded into a shotgun. Tom Burden had been taking a nap, apparently.

"You're not where you're supposed to be, Mr. Johnson."

I put my hands in the air, each holding one of the pictures. Taking the gun away from the bastard would be no problem. I wanted to hear his story first.

"Put those down." He directed me with the barrel of the Marlin.

I placed the photographs back on the stereo cabinet. "Guess we have a lot in common. Much more than some might say is appropriate."

"Shut your mouth." He stepped closer, shoved the shotgun into my chest. I grabbed the barrel, turned it away from me and yanked it out of his hands. I pointed it between his eyes. "Let's talk."

"You killed my little girl."

"She was dead long before she met me, bubba." No one could know how difficult it was to keep from splattering his skull and brains all over the walls. "So what happens when you get the patent to Seraphim?"

He refused to answer.

I cradled the gun in my right hand, picked up the picture of Lorraine as a teenager and threw it against the wall, shattering the glass frame it was contained in.

Dr. Burden gazed at the photo. Broken glass protected it from careless hands. "You don't understand," he choked, like he might try to drop some pathetic tears. "I come from Tennessee. We have a different way of life."

I yawned without closing my eyes.

"Where I come from, everybody knows their place. Niggers, gooks, spics, and especially, your own children."

"That's tough," I said. "You might try selling a sensitive sob story like that to *National Geographic*, see if you can make a buck or two. Then again, in a few weeks, you'll have more money than you'll ever need, won't you?"

Dr. Burden stood silent, defiant. It reminded me of worthless arguments I had many a night with his daughter.

"What happens when you buy the patent to Seraphim?"

He grinned. "You're smarter than I gave you credit for," he said. "I invented Seraphim. Because I did it on Daisy time, they owned the initial rights. They, well, Leonard Black, didn't understand the promise of Seraphim, the ultimate goal."

"Which was?"

"Utopia, Mr. Johnson. Man has searched for decades and the answer has been here all along." He nodded toward the kitchen. "Might you be so kind as to allow me to show you my response to misery?"

I agreed, raising the shotgun to remind him how miserable things would get if he tried anything stupid.

We made our way through the kitchen, out the door and into the backyard. He led me right up to the poppy.

"They almost got it right in China," he explained. "You can see the uniformity, as I call it, in their work ethic. There are no individuals in China because they understand that man is not an island. He never was meant to be."

"You saying there's opium in Seraphim?"

"Oh no, no, that would bring so much red tape and legal fireworks from the FDA, no boy, that's not the point. The goal of Manifesto Destination is to take this failed social experiment called the United States of America and turn the population into an organic machine. This country is going to fall apart if we do not establish a cultural identity that overcomes this selfish need we have for recognizing differences between people from Asia and people from Africa and people from Australia and, well, you get the point. America has no unified culture. Seraphim will change that."

"I see." I started stepping away from the good doctor on the presumption that whatever disease screwed up his mind could get airborne.

"It sounds horrific now, but I challenge you to upset the good people who have embraced Seraphim's calming effects. It can't be done. As America becomes a service country, these folks will gladly do routine work that pays the bills and keeps a television set running in their houses."

"What's Leo Black's involvement in all this?"

He laughed. "What is any CEO's involvement? He appears on commercials with Don Marsh and other local celebrities. He hands out giant checks to hospitals. I tell him to donate to Manifesto Destination, he asks if it can be written off on his taxes. I tell him to donate space for research on illegal drugs such as, oh, I don't know, say, ah, Stardust, and he says fine, pours himself a shot of Cognac and rests his head on the back of a plush red comforter in his castle outside the city."

"So you ask him, 'Can I manufacture and distribute Stardust,' and he says, what?"

"Mr. Johnson, in a corporation the size of Daisy, you can make bombs and set them off and nobody will know anything about it. You give one task to one department,

140

another task to a different area, put it all together and call it something else on paper. Nobody ever has the beginning of a notion as to what's actually taking place. Paranoid folks refer to that sort of arrangement as a conspiracy, but it's nothing more than a good old fashioned bureaucracy."

I must have looked as confused as I was, because he continued in a condescending voice:

"Elmore, do you know how desperate the people who work for a living in this country are for relief? They'll start with a drink. The more adventurous, the more miserable, will tamper with marijuana, maybe try cocaine. Sooner or later, they will take the strongest medicine available. That just happens to be Stardust. When word gets out that the only cure for the drug's long-term effects is Seraphim, Daisy will run the country."

I wanted to ask, but didn't, who got the bulk of the profits from the Stardust operation at Daisy. It had to be the benevolent doctor. That's how he was going to outbid Leonard Black when it came time to auction off Seraphim's patent.

"You can't stop it, Elmore. Who would ever believe that a corporation that size would risk their neck operating a drug ring? That sort of story makes for good reading in tabloids, but the mainstream press would never touch it."

I backed toward my car. When I was far enough away, I tossed the shotgun into the tall grass. Maybe it would inspire the doctor to use some of his coming fortune to purchase a lawn mower.

41

I drove north. Leonard Black was innocent, for the most part. Maybe he had abandoned Felicia, if she really was blood kin. That was bad, but as long as men wrote the laws of the land, it wasn't a crime. His cab company was crooked, and he surely had some vague notion of that, but there isn't a taxi outfit in the nation that's on the level, so I could hardly hold that against him.

As I pulled into the long driveway leading to Leo's house, I got a sick feeling again. There was a stretch limo in the driveway and deep tire tracks in a mud patch by the front door. Someone had pulled right up to the steps, taken care of business and then peeled out.

With Lorraine in my hand, I approached the porch. The goons who greeted me the last time I showed up uninvited failed to welcome me.

The door was wide open. On the staircase just inside the main hallway, two of Leo's body guards were draped over one another. Gashes caused by bullets decorated their foreheads. It'd have made for a good picture if I had remembered to bring my camera.

I stepped into the living room. The big man was on his belly. The same as Aaron Milton. The same as Margie Crumb. A gunshot wound showed me what the back of his brains looked like. There was a .38, just like mine, near his feet. His body had fallen onto and shattered a glass coffee table. Among the shards on the floor was a note. I picked it up and read it. It was my kind of literature:

To hell with everybody!

It was signed "Leonard Black," but it was written in a dainty handwriting—Heather's, if she had indeed authored the notes in my apartment. Before I could deconstruct that little bit of what the college kiddies called "sudden fiction," two police officers stumbled through the front door, gathered in the refreshing sight of three dead bodies, pulled their guns and then shouted:

"On the floor! Now!"

There's a reason people don't like cops. Being yelled at and humiliated was a big chunk of why.

42

They carried me off in a paddy wagon with an eighteen-year-old yuppie punk who told me his name was "OG Trey."

"I keep it real up at the Four Seasons, G'." He nodded after every sentence, as though his own words slapped him in the jaw.

"Is there any danger of things being unreal at your country club?" I asked him.

"Yo, G'," he said. The kid looked like his parents raked a hundred grand a year. In Indianapolis, that was a short way around the definition of rich. "You tryin' ta be smort, or sum'pin?"

I felt sorry for him. He must have been extremely unhappy to put on such a show. "Who hurt you, kid?"

"Can't nobody hurt me. I'm the hoidest nigga' in my 'hood."

"Where's that?"

"Beaver Creek Condominiums, cracker."

By that point, I was ready to laugh until my ribs fell out. The dork was a nice source of amusement in between all the nonsense I had been through. "Tough neighborhood, I hear."

"*Sheeee*-yat," he said. "Your Moms and Pops don't

buy you a fresh hooptie' every year, you might as well take the schoo' bus, know what I'm saying?"

"I sure don't." I thought he could use some cheering up with a little humor himself—"Hook me up with some Latin."

"Nigga'!" He must have thought mispronouncing the word somehow made it acceptable. "Don't make me beat dat' ass."

Anybody intent on kicking my ass wouldn't say a thing. They'd just do it. "What they get you for?" I asked.

"Yo', man, they said I was stealing a pack o' bref' mints from the Quality Drugs on a hun'erd and sixteenf', but they just trippin'."

"I see."

The brave white "gangsta" was silent for a moment, considering whether or not he should return the question. Then he shrugged, figured he could handle it. "How 'bout you, dawg?"

"They caught me standing over three bodies. Each one of them had holes in their heads from a .38." I made sure I had his attention. "You ever kill anybody?"

He shifted in his seat. He turned away before responding. "Heeel' yeah. What'you think, I'm frontin' o'sump'in?"

I didn't say another word.

43

Downtown they shuffled me through the system, put me in temporary, a lock-up so sadistic they installed windows in the tank for prisoners to get a good view of the arena the Pacers played ball in. Every Joe in there tried to shake me down for a cigarette. It was annoying. It was also safer than my apartment. Despite a voice nagging me to keep my heart just as cold as a stone, I worried about Felicia. They gave me a phone call and I used it to check up on her.

"You're in jail?" The shock in her voice sounded forced.

"Yes ma'am." I warded off a mute trying to sell me a dead mouse. "Murder. Leo Black. Looks like you and daddy will never have that tearful reunion talk shows like putting together."

"Do you need someone to bail you out?"

That hit me like a brick to the face. "I don't think that's possible, baby. Thanks for offering. I want you to promise me you won't go anywhere, understand? Some horrible things are headed around the mountain."

"I promise."

I hung up and returned to the saintly community of criminals gathered in the tank. An old man noticed I was fidgeting like I needed a cigarette. I didn't, but when he offered a drag on a Kool he had beaten down a teenager for, I accepted.

Whoever set me up decided to put me through what they no doubt considered hell. I had been in lock-up before, though, and didn't find it much worse than my own apartment. Or life, for that matter. I used half a roll of toilet paper for a pillow, crawled into a corner with my hands in my pockets and slept like a toddler.

44

The next day I was escorted by two suits from vice to the City-County Building. It felt good to be home. They dumped me in a room with a mirror along the far wall. I sat at a table taking up most of the space in the joint. Then they left.

The mirror was a two-way. Some schmuck stood on the other side, like a pervert, seeing how I reacted to various questions, making notes if I picked my nose.

A suit named Vincent, Detective Vincent Angelo, entered, introduced himself and sat down. Dressed in a blue shirt and black slacks, he looked like he was ready to go dancing at Eden or some other yuppie breeding hole. He carried a file under his arm and slid it across the table.

"That's a pretty heavy case. What's your plan?"

"How stupid do I look?"

"You shot a man in the back of head and then tried to pass it off as a suicide."

Trust me, I smiled. "The note isn't in my handwriting."

"That can be arranged." He ran his fingers through his greased up hair. "I'll have my senior talk with you."

He stood and left. The file was still in front of me. I knew there was a crew of uniforms and suits standing outside the window waiting for a show, so I gave it to them.

Opening the manila folder, I saw that there was one piece of paper in it. In tiny, type-written letters, someone had come up with this piece of poetry:

Just Be Cool

I smirked, put the file back together and laid it down on the desk once more.

Then Jerome McElroy entered.

"You are one crazy bastard," he said. He was chewing tobacco, carrying a Dixie cup to spit in. As he sat down across from me he continued. "You know we could send you up, for good."

"And you know it'll never stick. Not in court."

"Who's going to believe you? A two-bit snoop? You don't even have a license to do what you do. On top of that, I got word that a follicle test would reveal some interesting things about you that would only enhance the DA's case."

"Dependants Anonymous?" I said.

Jerome shook his head. "Don't act stupid. I'm here to make a deal."

"All right. Let's make a deal." I folded my hands on the table and grinned like a politician.

"You go back to your office, wait for the next floozy who thinks her husband is cheating on her to call for some dirty pictures and forget all about the Magic Carpet."

"What do I get in return?"

That question baffled him. "Give me a break. You get to avoid a trial and execution for murder."

"What if I blow the whistle, again, show the DA pictures of Express Taxis doling out dope across the city?"

He grinned. "Why would that bother me?"

"Because I got a shot of the dealer walking into City-County to make a pay off."

We traded our best poker faces.

He sighed. "All I have to do is make a call and those photos and anything else you got in your apartment will be on my desk by the end of the day."

"Who said they were at my apartment?"

"OK. You gave them to your only friend, Felicia Hill. She works for us, dumbass. I can get them from her in even less time."

"If I, indeed, gave them to her."

Stalemate.

"What are you looking for?"

I leaned in and spoke in a lighter voice. If McElroy's colleagues outside couldn't hear him, I figured, he might be apt to cough up some answers. "What's your angle, just tell me that, for the sake of curiosity."

His eyes narrowed and he smirked in a manner suggesting he was proud of what he was about to say. "I got an offer, a very good offer, for the Magic Carpet. All I have to do is get certain people to cooperate."

"You and Tom Burden cozy?"

Jerome slammed his fist into the table. "That's all you get, Johnson." He stood and left.

After another period of peek-a-boo with the two-way glass, Vincent, the suit, entered the room once more.

"You're a free man. I suggest you stay as far away from here as possible."

Not likely, I thought. "Will do," I said.

45

After a bureaucratic waltz to get my car out of impound, a little dance that involved waiting in line at three different buildings across the city, I drove to Felicia's.

A Caddie was parked where I normally left my Towne Car. I was instinctively jealous. It was Abe Miller's. As much as I hated the thought of him putting his paws all over Felicia, the truth was, his presence there might have kept the county morgue free of one more "suicide."

I rang her buzzer. She answered and I could tell she was embarrassed to hear from me.

"Come on up." She must have realized I had already seen Prince Charming's pimp mobile out front.

Felicia opened the door, dressed only in a long T-shirt. Her hair was wet and she smelled like Irish Spring. From her bedroom, Abe Miller grunted.

"So this is what it was all about, eh?"

The big man shuffled out in his boxers. When he saw me he turned red. He snapped at Felicia. "Why didn't you tell me the snoop was coming over?"

"Sorry," she said. Her tone let me know there were

no feelings between her and the smut lord. Just in case I didn't pick up on it, she whispered, "It's only business."

Abe stomped back into the bedroom.

"You're a clever woman, Felicia." I moseyed to her kitchen, found an unopened bottle of Jack Daniels in the refrigerator door, opened it and took a swig.

"What makes you say that?" She crossed her arms, causing her T-shirt to hike up.

Seeing her thighs that early in the day made me take another drink. "You and Abe had me snap those pictures to keep the big boys from taking the Magic Carpet."

She stood still.

"Either you knew, or suspected, that McElroy had gotten involved with the Wizard of Daisy, Tom Burden. It was only a matter of time before the money from Stardust and other fine Daisy Products tempted Jerome to sell out the porno ring. But you and Abe weren't going to be in on that, so you did your best to put a dent in Daisy's expansion plans."

She raised her right brow.

"I got bad news, baby. You're up against a monster that's going to devour the whole town with or without your cooperation."

Abe returned, dressed in a white suit. He combed what nasty strands of hair he had left on his scalp. "Nice job, snoop," he said. "What the hell are we supposed to do?"

"Nothing."

"Forget it." He marched toward the door. Before leaving, he took a shot at a minor pissing contest with me by grabbing Felicia and attempting to kiss her.

She pushed him away.

"Fine," he said. He opened the door and stepped through, then turned around. "See if I keep them off your back any longer."

"You want to start watching your own back, bubba," I told him. He shut the door before I could finish.

"Great." Felicia went to the kitchen and made herself a glass of sludge she had grown used to calling water. When she returned I saw, for the first time, genuine fear in her eyes.

"How much money you got?"

"Um," she took a drink, thought about it. "I have seventeen grand saved up, in a locker-box in Tony's room."

"Can you go somewhere?"

"I have family in Louisiana."

When she said that, I got the notion I might not see her again. Sadness spilled through my bones. This was the woman I should have invested my heart in, not Lorraine. The way the wind blew, as Professor Keller would have put it, the way the stars were aligned, whatever fancy dressing you put on the term "fate," we would never live the life I knew both of us desired. We were too tough to admit we wanted to be happy. Circumstances wouldn't give us the chance to lighten up and take that sort of risk.

"Gather what you can. You and Tony go south and don't ever come back unless I tell you it's safe."

While she threw clothes and other items she thought important into a navy suitcase, I called for a taxi.

She filled it to capacity, sat on it, and snapped it shut. Then she found a smaller bag and went to work packing up Tony's clothes. I kneeled down and played Tonka trucks with the little man while his mother hustled to save both of their lives.

When she finished stuffing as much as she could into three different pieces of luggage, I carried them down the steps to the front walk. Felicia stood outside with Tony on her hip.

The taxi arrived and the driver hopped out, popped the trunk and rushed over to help us load her baggage. I handed him a hundred dollar bill. "Straight to the bus station. Don't dwell in traffic, don't get pulled over, and forget this ride ever happened."

The cabbie was a veteran. He wore a Colts baseball cap, hadn't shaved in a few days and worked on a Dutch Masters President, a cigar too fancy for my taste. He stuffed the money in his Hawaiian shirt, jumped in and roared away from 25th Street.

And Felicia Hill vanished from my life. I experienced the sort of heartache I imagined sappy women wrote about in magazines you see at the checkout lanes in supermarkets. Then I noticed I felt nauseous. I tried to figure out what could have upset me and then I remembered:

I didn't think anything of it when the cabbie shut the trunk. I was too concerned with making sure nobody saw Felicia and her boy get in the taxi. My emotions were getting all worked up because she was leaving once more and I had failed to tell her how I felt about her. Why, under those circumstances, would I have ever taken time to notice and, for that matter, give a rat's ass about the fact that the number on the taxi was none other than 525.

46

The cabbie flew down College and turned onto South Street. I tailed him in my Lincoln. At a corner a mile east of the bus depot, he pulled into a gas station. There was a convenience store one block down.

I ducked in and bought a pint of Jim Beam and new pack of Apaches. When I returned to my car, I saw the hack putting the finishing touches on a fresh tank of gas. I wanted to stroll over and strangle him. A hundred bucks for a twenty-dollar ride and he still couldn't follow my goddamn instructions.

He drove to the bus station across from the Hoosier Dome. I pulled to the curb at Capitol Avenue and watched. The taxi driver opened the door for Felicia and helped a porter take her luggage out of the trunk. I prayed she didn't tell him where she was going.

She hustled into the bus station and the porter loaded her suitcases on a cart and followed. The cabbie got back in his taxi and drove away.

For insurance, I followed him to his next ride. An old lady at the Circle Center mall hailed it. She got in, explained at length where needed to go, and 525 moved on.

The taxi turned onto Meridian and took the woman to the safety of the north side.

47

That night I decided to keep an eye on Abe Miller. Aside from myself, he was the last brick in the wall between the Magic Carpet and a world run by Daisy. Armed with my camera, Lorraine, Jim Beam and my cigars, I parked at the post office and observed the operation at the old Vonnegut Lofts. There were twice as many trucks loading up and scattering in different directions for I-70, I-74, I-69, and I-65. They didn't call Indianapolis "The Crossroads of America" for nothing.

Charlie Parker With Strings complemented the buzz I was building. I had an entire fifth with me and half was gone within thirty minutes. When I smoked an Apache, I got a head rush, the kind you get when you're thirteen and sneak a Marlboro out of your dad's dinner jacket.

I nearly fell asleep waiting for the strip club to close. Abe Miller walked out at a quarter past four. He was alone. A modern Chevy Caprice, white, pulled up to the sidewalk and stopped. Abe poked his snout into the passenger-side window.

The car parked and a blonde, packed tight in a black one-piece dress, snaked out of the driver's side.

Over the noise from the Daisy drones working across the street, I heard Abe say, as he put his arm around the blonde and led her back into the club, "Been a while!"

I stepped out of the Lincoln. There was a nice shadow between the post office and the streetlights. I used it to move closer to the Magic Carpet without anyone noticing.

Half a block away, I heard a gunshot. I stopped. The blonde hustled out. She glanced around and got in her car.

I ran back to mine, started it up and followed her. I already knew what kind of mess she left in the Magic Carpet.

The woman turned onto Madison Avenue and drove south. I hadn't gotten a good look at her face when she was outside the club, but I recognized her hips. She drove into Beech Grove and parked, not much to my surprise, near Jerome McElroy's fancy shithole. I pulled to a curb and turned my engine off.

Nurse Heather corkscrewed in her little dress right up to McElroy's front door. She knocked and waited.

Jerome stepped out, shouted something over his shoulder and shut the door. Heather leaned in and whispered in his ear. They embraced and traded spit for a minute longer than "just friends."

I put the 250 on the Pentax and took some sentimental pictures.

48

After Jerome and Heather dry-humped on his stoop for ten minutes or so, Heather kissed him goodbye and jumped back into her car.

I followed her as she turned onto Keystone and headed north.

She passed downtown and I got an inkling as to where she was going. The fifth was almost empty, but I didn't have time to stop and buy a new bottle. To make matters worse, just before we crossed Fall Creek and officially entered the north side of town, my Charlie Parker tape got stuck and then eaten. "Stella by Starlight" quickly went from ballad to manic anthem to silence.

At 54th Street, Heather turned left and then right when she got to Broadway. When she pulled up in front of Tom Burden's house, the deck was in my corner. I hurried home to develop the shots of the nurse and police officer getting cozy.

49

The next day I paid a visit to Dr. Thomas Burden at his home. I knocked on the door. Over and over again, until he got out of bed and answered.

"What do you want?" He hadn't shaved yet and looked like a man who once envisioned the world dropping into his palms.

"I don't know why it took me so long to figure this out," I said. "I guess you and Heather are an item, no?"

"What does that have to do with anything?"

"You got a will?"

He nodded.

"She get the goodies when you pass?"

He didn't say anything. He didn't need to.

I showed him a photograph of Heather and the cop. "I feel bad about ruining the picture of you and your daughter the other day. Maybe you can put this one up on the mantle."

Dr. Burden stared at the tender shot of his sweetheart cleaning off McElroy's mouth with her tongue. "Come on in," he said.

He led me to the dining room. Dr. Burden put the mannequin on the floor and pointed to the empty seat. Then he sat down on the opposite side of the table.

"After I get the patent for Seraphim," he began, "I'll eventually have enough to buy Daisy. Heather and I have been married longer than my plans to take over the company have existed. She had me write the will, said it would guarantee nobody would stand in the way of our Utopia. I thought I could trust her."

"Pretty girls aren't made to be trusted, doc." I pulled a cigar out of my jacket.

"No smoking in this house."

I lit it anyway, dropped ashes on the floor. "I don't have much sympathy for you, Tom. You ruined the woman I was in love with, messed her up real good before I even met her."

"That's slander."

"Shut the hell up," I said. "Your little bunny Heather is going to kill you. You know that. What's the clause in your will?"

"When I die, she gets it all. It doesn't matter how it happens."

"Too bad, for you, bubba. She's got a habit of helping folks shoot themselves in the back of the head."

"That's between her and McElroy. My method for getting rid of trouble, well, you should know…"

"And I appreciate the fact that you only tried to kill my soul. Much better to be a vegetable, alive and well, working on the railroad."

The front door opened and in walked the little lady. She saw me, sneered at Tom, then reached into her purse and pulled out a .22.

"Well, look who's here," I said.

She grabbed the picture in Tom's hands. Her head twitched and she laughed as she dropped the photo onto the table. "Big deal," she said. "What does it prove? Nothing."

"It proves one thing." I stood up.

Heather faced me, just long enough for Dr. Burden to make a move for her pistol. She was quicker than the old goat and shot him in the face.

She turned the gun on me, but I already had Lorraine in my hand, itching to spit a slug in her belly.

"You messed up, doll. How you going to pass this off as a suicide?"

She didn't answer. Neither did she drop the gun.

"Why shoot me?" I asked her. "There's nothing left to gain."

"But you know everything." She raised her .22.

As soon as I saw her hand move I let a bullet fly into the floor between her feet. She dropped her pistol and gawked at me like I was a monster. I grabbed her arm and yanked her to my side.

"Here's how it is, baby," I said. "We're going down to the DA's, as in the District Attorney, and you're gonna sit at a table and soak it with tears. Lucky for you, the DA is a man. A stupid man. He'll fall for a sob story about Jerome talking you into all this and make a deal with you. You put McElroy behind bars and you get to walk, sound reasonable?"

"But I love..."

I stopped her. "That might work on anyone else in the world, but not me. I've seen firsthand your talent to play one role right into the next. You know damn well once McElroy pulled his weight to clear your name after all the murders, after all the money was in your pocket, you were going to get rid of him, too."

She struggled. I tightened my grip on her arm. The look in her eyes told me she was in physical pain. I wasn't too concerned.

"Maybe not murder, because you need him to gloss over the reports in the morgue, no, but you would have given him the eighty-six somehow. Frankly, it doesn't matter now."

I dragged her by her arm to my car and drove her downtown. I smoked cigars the whole way and refused to crack a window.

50

Days passed. *The Indianapolis Star* jumped all over the story of corruption at IPD and Daisy and the Magic Carpet. It was all for nothing, though, because the ink and paper had already set the wheels in motion. Daisy bought the Magic Carpet and tore it down. I drove by the old Vonnegut Lofts to see if the Stardust operation had slowed. There were trucks leaving the building every other minute.

Within time, the national press reported on a new drug epidemic spreading across the nation. In between the newscasts tugging fears with the horror stories authored by Stardust, commercials advertised the wonders of Seraphim. It could cure depression, anxiety, and drug addiction. A miracle, thought many.

Bullshit, thought I.

While waiting for Felicia to call, I came to the conclusion that snooping wasn't my business. I gathered together twelve of my best photographs and made what the artsy folks called a portfolio.

I threw copies of the pictures in my trunk and drove to the fancy mall at Keystone and 86th Street. There was a Barnes and Noble and a Borders at the bourgeois shopping temple. Between them, I figured I could find a book with a list of production companies who might need a set photographer.

"This is what I'm going to do with my life," I told the sky. The part of me that refused to grow up imagined Lorraine, in heaven, gazing down and, perhaps, being pleased with my decision to do something seemingly less sleazy for a living.

I returned home and proceeded to pimp my work to the flakes out in Hollywood. Gazing at the empty apartment directly across from mine, I sealed a dozen envelops, adding a vacant prayer to each stamp I slapped on the outside.

51

The last grand from the ten Felicia gave me for the Marsha Blank gig was almost gone. Something needed to come through, soon. I got a note from the post office, the branch across from the Vonnegut Lofts. A registered letter had been sent there.

I drove the Lincoln down Meridian, noticing artificial smiles at the steering wheels of every car at every traffic light. If Seraphim had an odor, I thought, the air reeked of it.

As I drove past Monument Circle and entered what was officially the south side of town, I noticed that most of the land had been cleared and fenced off. A bulldozer sat where the Magic Carpet once entertained horny bastards, rich or poor. It made me sad to see the big fish win.

Nothing mattered to me in Indianapolis. The registered letter, I was sure, was an invitation to fly out west and start a new life. This time, I promised myself, I'd wait until I got to Los Angeles to have a drink.

I stood in line at the post office. When I got to the window, an older gal with a round face and giant square glasses took the notice from me and disappeared behind a door to a room made of cubicle walls.

She returned with a mid-sized envelope and asked me to sign an invoice stuck to the outside. "There you go."

52

I waited until I was in my car to open the letter. I had a pint of Jim Beam in the glove box, next to an Apache. I lit the cigar and cracked the bottle. After three swigs of whiskey, I set the booze down and tore the perforated edges on the envelope.

A slit in the narrow side parted and I pulled out a folded piece of green paper, an official notice of some sort. A sticky note was attached to it that read, simply,

For your information

I unfolded the green paper. It was a birth certificate. Felicia Vanessa Hill, it stated, had been born on that day, November 16, 1969. Her mother had signed her name, Francis Janine Hill. The father's name was typed in with a doctor's signature underneath, next to a notary public stamp.

Her father's name was Leonard Walter Black.

"Son of a bitch." I tossed the certificate onto the passenger seat. I drove to the only place I could go. Halfway back to my apartment, the goddamn bottle was dry again.

Alec Cizak is a writer and filmmaker from Indiana. His work has appeared in several journals and anthologies. He is the author of three novellas, *Down on the Street*, *Between Juarez and El Paso*, and *Manifesto Destination*. He is also the chief editor of the fiction digest *Pulp Modern*.

nomoralcenter.blogspot.com/

On the following pages are a few
more great titles from the
Down & Out Books publishing family.

For a complete list of books and to
sign up for our newsletter,
go to DownAndOutBooks.com.

Exacting Justice
The De La Cruz Case Files
TG Wolff

Down & Out Books
March 2018
978-1-946502-50-6

Assigned the case of a gruesome—and very public—series of murders is Cleveland Homicide Detective Jesus De La Cruz, a former undercover narcotics cop and a recovering alcoholic. The cost of progress is more than he bargained for. Demands from his superiors, grief of the victims' relatives, pressure from the public, and stress from his family quietly pull him apart. With no out, Cruz moves all in, putting his own head on the line to bait a killer.

Abnormal Man
Grant Jerkins

ABC Group Documentation,
an imprint of Down & Out Books
September 2016
978-1-943402-39-7

Chaos? Or fate? What brought you here? Were the choices yours, or did something outside of you conspire to bring you to this place? Because out in the woods, in a box buried in the ground, there is a little girl who has no hope of seeing the moon tonight. The moon has forsaken her. Because of you.

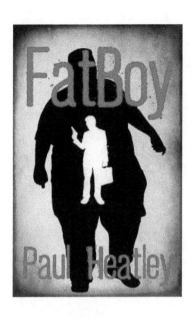

Fatboy
Paul Heatley

All Due Respect, an imprint of
Down & Out Books
978-1-946502-94-0

Is Joey Hidalgo really as angry, as volatile, so close to constant violence, as ex-girlfriend claims he is? No, Joey thinks, of course not, the real problem is money—or lack thereof. Joey's a bartender, always struggling to make ends meet, unlike his most vile regular customer, the rich and racist fatboy. So Joey hatches a plan to get his family back by taking him for all he's worth.

But the fatboy isn't going to make it easy for them. Neither is Joey's temper. Things are going to get messy, and it's gonna be one hell of a long night.

Slaughterhouse Blues
A Love & Bullets Hookup
Nick Kolakowski

Shotgun Honey, an imprint of
Down & Out Books
February 2018
978-1-946502-40-7

Holed up in Havana, Bill and Fiona know the Mob is coming for them. But they're not prepared for who the Mob sends: a pair of assassins so utterly amoral and demented, their behavior pushes the boundaries of sanity. Seriously, what kind of killers pause in mid-hunt to discuss the finer points of thread count and luxury automobiles? If they want to survive, our fine young criminals can't retreat anymore: they'll need to pull off a massive (and massively weird) heist—and the loot has some very dark history...

CPSIA information can be obtained
at www.ICGtesting.com
Printed in the USA
BVHW03020426061 9
551992BV00013B/41/P

9 781946 502964